AF254699

Short Tall Tales

Bryan Clark

SHORT TALL TALES Written by Bryan Clark

First Edition: December 2019

ISBN 13: 9781733801027 – Short Tall Tales (paperback)
ISBN 10: 1733801022 (paperback)

ISBN 13: 9781714069170 – Short Tall Tales (hardcover)
ISBN 13: 9781733801034 – Short Tall Tales (eBook)

Cover Design by Bryan Clark and Pixelstudio

For my children, grandchildren, and some friends

TABLE OF CONTENTS

Jeremiah And the Mule

I been around mules all my life and I ain't never had no trouble with 'em; well, almost never. What I think confuses your everyday fella is that they think a mule is stupid, but they're talking through their hat. In fact, there is probably some mules smarter than some people, but I learned early on that not too many people want to hear that; 'specially the dumb ones. I grew up on a tobacco farm, and my Paw and older brother and I had us four pretty fine mules. We would a been hurting a lot if we didn't have no mules to pull the planter, and it would a taken twice as many horses to haul the picked tobacco leaves from the fields into the barn. No, sir, mules were the ticket.

When the war come, Paw said he was too old for that stuff, but me and my older brother, Solomon, walked on over to Murfreesboro and joined the Army of the Confederacy. What I thought was pretty weird was that there was a soldier right across the street that was enlisting fellas for the Union army. Don't that seem strange? They said they wouldn't take no boys under twelve, even though I was near six feet tall already, so I told 'em I was twelve and Solomon swore to it, so we both got in. I didn't, honest to God, know how old I was, so I might have been twelve at the time, but they wouldn't give me no gun anyway when they found out I could drive a mule team, even though I was by far the youngest driver they had. When we had big loads on the farm, Paw always had me drive the team, but that was only two; the Army teams was six and they were a little different to steer, with a set of reins on the pole mules and another set for the smaller lead pair. But it was just a question of me learning how much teaching they needed and them learning who was boss.

The next few years were a pretty good education for me: I don't mean like from books or like that, but it's just that I saw a lot of how bloody war was and how different fellas reacted in very different ways. I found out for sure that you can't tell much about a fella by how he looks or how he talks, you got to wait and see how he acts when it matters, and that'll tell you who he is. I saw more than one fella throw himself in the line of fire to save another fella, and not even his brother; I don't think that kind of thing is in me, but it sure made a powerful impression on me that there are really people like that walking around right here in the middle of us all. I've been slow to judge, ever since.

Mules are maybe a little more skittish than horses, so I hauled a lot of ammunition but never as far up as the front lines, because the mules would probly go crazy with all that cannon fire. I hauled a lot of officers' gear, and I hauled a lot of food supplies, and one trip, they loaded a bunch of coffins on us and I hauled 'em all back to Savannah. I seen a fair amount of the country, into Georgia and both Carolinas and as far north as Virginia, but not for long. Even with all the fires and destruction and the men getting maimed and all, there's a lot of it that is mighty pretty, but I didn't see nothing that would make me want to leave Tennessee.

A few years down the line, I was driving my team back to base one afternoon, and my sergeant called up to me and said, "Boy, get down off that rig; we're going home!" I asked him what day it was, and he said, "It's April 10th, 1865, fool, – Lee quit it yesterday." I didn't realize it had been going on that long. We was somewhere on a farmhouse north of Rome, Georgia then, so I was going to have a pretty long walk home, but I took two of the pole mules with me. Nobody seemed to mind, so I got to ride near all the way; I cut into northern Alabama 'cause I didn't want to come through any of those raggedy passes into Tennessee.

Coming home wasn't near as good as I had expected. Paw had fallen off one of the drying pegs in the tobacco barn and went lame, and Solomon didn't come home at all; didn't nobody tell us, but we figured he was probly in that mess up in Gettysburg. From then on, I was pretty much running the farm, or what was left of it, and I decided that tobacco was more than a little hard for one man to handle, so I talked Paw into helping me breed mules. I knew there was a lot of them killed off during the war: I had a lead pair blowed up right in front of me. So, I figured the market near home should be pretty good. We had us a couple of mares, so then we took the proceeds of that year's tobacco crop and bought us a flock of donkeys, and we started coupling them, and it weren't long 'fore we were touted as the place to get the best mules in the whole county.

It was my idea about breeding them, so Paw let me name 'em. I started at the top of the alphabet and decided to leave out all the vowels and the Q and X because you want a sharp single sound for a mule's name, so he knows right away who you're talking to. I started with Abe and Ben and Cal and Duke and Fess and went all the way through to Sam, Tad, Vick and Zeb by the time I was probly twenty. I was pretty much living and breathing with mules by then, and that was the year that Paw took pneumonia and died, and a year later, Maw went after him; I think mostly through loneliness. So, for quite a few years after, it was just me and the mules, so that's pretty much why everyone around figures I understand mules better than anybody else they seen. Now I can't argue with that and have no mind to, but it comes with some problems because you know how stories get started and you know how some people just can't seem to leave the simple truth alone; they got to add all kinds of curly-cues to it? Well one of the things that is pretty widely passed around these parts is that I can talk to mules. Well, you remember me telling you that there is probably some mules that is smarter than some people? Well – these are the people I was talking about. Mules are smart, and I'm the last one who would deny it; they won't let nobody work 'em to death like a dumb old horse will, and they won't go into anything they think is dangerous to them; that's what most people think is stubbornness, but I call it just good sense. But that don't mean that you can talk regular sentences to them and it sure as the dickens don't mean they can understand a lot of words. That's just a pile of horse pucky.

I got to admit, though, that I had one mule from out of the second alphabet crop that I named Gus, that had somehow picked up a few of a dog's traits. He would sometimes follow me around when I was feeding and stick his muzzle in my hand even when I didn't have no feed there. One time, he was walking aside me through some high grass, and he jumped ahead of me and reared up and stomped down real quick, and when I took a good look, he had stomped on a rattler that was right in my path. Not usual for a mule to go anywhere near danger. He came out a little frail, and I had to kind a nurse him through the first four months or so, and I got to admit, I probably had a special interest in him after I spent so much time with him as a little tyke. Even when he got full grown and healthy, I just somehow was not in the mood to let him go, so I just kept him around, and he was the one I mostly rode. Sometimes, I admit, I would talk to him like you talk to your dog, but that don't mean I thought he could understand me.

It still surprises me how many farmers there are who have good mules and don't have no idea how to treat 'em. I used to try and tell a fella who was buying one of our mules how to handle him, but there is an awful lot of grown men who don't think that a youngster can tell them anything about anything; so, after a while I just gave up, and that turned out to be a good thing for me, and I'll tell you how. Now, when a farmer has a problem with his mule, he comes looking for me to fix it, so somehow, I pretty much become a mule "doctor." Here's how I work it: if he brings me the mule, I will fix him for a dollar; if I have to go to his farm, it costs him two dollars. 'Course I never let the fella see exactly what I'm doing; I take the mule out behind a barn or something, and all the time we're walking away I got a holt of his ear, and I'm acting like I'm talking to him. Hey, if they don't want to listen to me when I'm trying to give 'em free advice, let 'em pay for it. And, of course the most sensitive part of a mule is his ears, so as soon as I grab that ear, he has a pretty good idea that I'm the boss and that it would be a good idea for him to pay attention. Just 'cause folks want to believe a lot of foolish prattle, don't blame me.

It's not like it's only a bunch of dumb farmers who fall for that kind of stuff. Reverend Brandywine stopped me on the street downtown one time when I was coming out of the feed store and wanted to talk to me about how Jesus rode into Jerusalem on an ass and did I think that Jesus and the ass had a conversation? Now, this is supposedly a educated man who is instructing the town folks on how to live their lives and stuff, and here he is, just as dumb as soap. First of all, an ass is not a mule, it's a whole other species or something – it's a donkey or a burro, it's not a mule; and secondly, how can you possibly believe that some poor animal can talk to people? I ended up thinking, maybe not all the asses are in the Bible, some of them are walking around right here in town.

Wild tales about my special abilities is not the only thing that resulted from me being all alone with a bunch of mules; there wasn't a woman within twenty miles that would even go to a barn dance with me. Now I know as well as any farmer that livestock of any kind tends to share its odor with you, especially if you're with 'em fourteen hours a day, but it's not as if I didn't bathe at all; I did every Saturday just like Maw and Paw did – well almost every one, but certainly if I was going into one of the stores in town or if I heard of a barn dance that was far enough away. Also, I was getting good money for my mules and had traded off our two old mares for a couple of prime fillies and had collected a new batch of donkeys to replace the old ones. The farm was making more money than Paw had ever made, and there was just me and one hired hand, Rufus Clay, so I was in pretty good shape for money, but that still didn't seem to attract the kind of flies I wanted to be buzzing around me. I didn't spend all my time worrying about it, but over the next few years it was beginning to occur to me that I could end up on this farm all by myself – except for a bunch of mules.

It was somewhere about then that Abbie Dalton rode in on a really smooth looking grey mare to see if I would sell her a good pair of mules. Well, I asked her to come on up on the porch and set a spell while I washed my hands, and I got her a glass of iced tea and went in and tried to make myself look presentable; I also sprinkled myself all over with Paw's old Bay Rum in the hope that it would tone down the mule smell. Oh yeah, I know that was dumb, but if you were a guy and you worked a farm, and Abbie Dalton rode up to your place, I guar-ran-damn-tee-you, you would be doing something just as stupid to spruce yourself up. If she wasn't the prettiest widow in the county, I don't know who was. She used to be Abbie Crabgrass, but she married old Aaron Dalton some years back when she was just a slip of a girl, and now old Dalton had just recently passed on to his "reward," as they say. My take on it was that he had plenty of reward right here being married to Abbie.

I showed her the two best mules I had, and I took my time about it, because I didn't know when I would ever be this close to a pretty woman again, not that I actually got very close, but you know what I mean. She didn't seem repulsed by me, so maybe the Bay Rum was doing its job, and she asked a couple of sensible questions about feed and caring for them. Actually, they will eat almost anything, but whatever you feed your horses or your cattle you can feed them, and I explained in great detail about a mule's ears and how if you have even a regular buggy whip you can get them to obey pretty well with not much fuss or bother. Mine are all taught Gee, Haw, Whoa, and Scud before they leave the farm.

It all seemed to go pretty well, right up until she said she'd take them and asked me if I could cart them over to the Dalton place tomorrow. Well of course I could, but I had never taken money from a woman before in my life, and somehow I got sort of tongue-tied and I was moving my arms around like a crazy person and I threw my left hand back and stuck it on the barbed-wire fence, and when I pulled it off, there was blood all over the place. She was just great; she took my bloody hand and pulled a handkerchief out of her bag and wrapped it up and made me hold it over my head, and walked me over to the pump and washed it and kind of patted it dry. I was making a bigger fool of myself during all this by trying to tell her not to bother, and she kept shushing me, and finally she put her little tiny hand over my big fat mouth. I can't explain that feeling, but it was not like anything I can ever remember feeling before; it had been over ten years since my Maw died and that was the last person who had ever touched me with anything like what you might call "tenderness," and this was definitely not my Maw. I was pretty speechless; she didn't have to cover my mouth anymore, but I wished she would; I wished she would just touch me again … sometime before I die.

She put the money in one hand and made me promise to put a bandage on the other and said to come by tomorrow any time after noon and rode off on her lucky grey mare. I don't know what I had for dinner that night, or even whether I ate, but I could remember every second of the time she was on my farm. I couldn't get to sleep that night and ended up setting on the porch and waking up with the cock crow the next morning, so I must have slept some. I washed those two mules and brushed them and even trimmed their ears, and I probly would have painted them if I thought it would help, then I washed me and brushed me and trimmed my beard and my ear hairs and my nose hairs and my fingernails, and it's a wonder I didn't cut off something of value in all the excitement. And finally … it was noon.

Aaron Dalton had a nice spread, not huge, but a well-planned variety: some peach trees and some pear trees and a half-dozen apples, and he had about ten rows of grape up on the hillside at the back of the property and still about twenty acres left for corn and beans and tomatoes. He must of left it in pretty good shape because he had been dead over two years now and it still looked to be healthy, or else, maybe Miss Abbie knew what she was doing and had hired the right kind of caretakers. She was out by the barn when I pulled up in the cart with the two mules in the back, and she waved me over right away. She had a kind of blue apron pinned on the front of her dress, and she had on work gloves, and there were two handymen standing by so we got the mules down with no trouble Then one of the hands got a yoke off the barn wall and come up behind Jeb, the smaller mule, and was going to slip it on him. Now that's okay for horses and maybe other animals, but you don't want to come up behind a mule with anything that clinks and clanks. Jeb heard something behind him that might be dangerous, and he reared up them hind legs and kicked that young fella about six feet through the air right into the side of the barn. I guess I should a warned him, but it never occurred to me that any farmhand wouldn't have learned not to walk up behind a mule's ass. Abbie ran over to him and patted his chest and held his face in her arms and talked real nice to him and in a couple of minutes he came out of it and he could stand up and walk, so I guess he was okay, and, in fact, he had learned a valuable lesson, and he also got held in Abbie Dalton's arms for a few minutes, so I think he could count it a pretty good day after all.

We were having iced tea on her front porch, a real polite little colored girl had brought us a big pitcher with ice in it, and Miss Abbie had unpinned her apron and was in a simple, pink-colored farm dress that looked real nice on her. She was telling me she was looking forward to using the mules for fall harvest and for spring planting next year, and I told her if there was anything else I could do for her, I'd sure be much obliged if she'd just let me know. She just took a long sip on her tea then, so I figured that was probly my cue to shut my trap and head for home, so I stood up and grabbed my hat, but then she said, "Well, Jeremiah, there is one little thing," so I sat down real quick.

"Jeremiah, you know Mr. Dalton's been dead over two years now?"

"Yes'm, I'm awful sorry for your loss."

"Well, thank you, Jeremiah, but what I want to ask you about was what your feelings were on the subject of the mourning period."

"Well, Ma'am … I don't rightly know how I feel about that."

"Well, I was talking to Pricilla Whitehouse after church last Sunday, and she suggested that two years was quite an acceptable period. Would you agree with that estimate, Jeremiah?"

"Oh … well, Yes, Ma'am, if that's what Missus Whitehouse says."

"Well then, you wouldn't see anything untoward about my having a barn dance here sometime in the near future, would you, Jeremiah?"

"Oh, no, Ma'am, not at all."

"Oh good, I'm so relieved, Jeremiah."

"Yes, Ma'am."

"There's just one more thing."

"Yes'm?"

"Would you consider being my escort if I find a convenient time for you?"

"Your escort, Ma'am?"

"Yes – would that be something you could do for me, Jeremiah?"

"Well, Ma'am … I, uh … I …

"If I said 'please,' Jeremiah?"

"My goodness, Ma'am … yes … I'd be … I'd be … pleased as punch."

"That's very sweet of you, Jeremiah."

"Oh, no, Ma'am … not at all."

"And just one other, tiny little thing …?"

"Anything at all, Ma'am, anything at all."

"Jeremiah, would you please call me Abbie?"

"Oh – well, yes Ma'am … I mean … yes … Abbie."

"Thank you, Jeremiah, that's awfully sweet of you … now, would you like some more iced tea?"

I don't remember much after that until I looked up and saw a big half-moon peeking over the roof of my barn, and I was on the road driving my cart just about a quarter-mile from home, and it must have been pretty late at night. Mrs. Dalton – I mean, Abbie – had invited me to stay for supper, and I'm sure it was just great, and I think there was some Elderberry wine poured out, and I'm pretty sure that she played the piano in the parlor afterward, and I have a kind strong recollection that, just before she sent me home, she kissed her fingers and then put them same fingers on my lips. I don't see how I could make up a thing like that, do you?

I can't remember nothing … I mean anything, much about my childhood that was pleasant – and if it wasn't for Grandma Bessie I probably wouldn't even know how to read and write, because "school" was pretty much an afterthought for Ma and Pa. But Grandma Bessie would always correct my grammar, and she gave me my first book. I guess, in looking back, I can't blame them a lot because farming is a hard life, no matter what anybody tells you. I know Pa worked hard until the day he died, and it's true we always had food on the table, but it's not as if all of us kids didn't work full time from the day we could carry water. Ma was so hemmed in by planting and weeding and then canning and pickling that she was more like a servant than a mother, and I think she took it as a relief when she died.

Being a girl sure didn't help. The boys at least got store-bought pants and shirts, but almost everything I wore was made out of potato or grain sacks. My older brother, Jesse, was always grabbing my breasts from the time I was about thirteen until I hit him in his privates with a short two-by-four … and with him and two younger brothers the idea of "privacy" was only something I read about in books … when I could run away to the town library and find an hour to read by myself. When Pa told me that old man Dalton wanted to marry me, I thought that might be my way out of this hardscrabble existence, and by then Grandma Bessie was gone, so I didn't feel like anybody in this household had much of a care for me.

Well, old man Dalton wasn't a bad person, but his farmer's hands were as rough as tree bark, and that first night with him I thought I would cry my throat raw. He didn't expect a lot, which was all good for me, and I found out real soon that he probably hadn't had much tenderness in his life, because with just the smallest show of affection I could get him to do practically anything, and I could most often satisfy him and still keep him off of me; most of the time. My life changed a lot for the better, but my "childhood" was certainly a thing of the past.

After the war, there were an awful lot of coloreds living on the edge of town who didn't have a master anymore and really didn't have any kind of jobs. They were living hand to mouth on their best day, so I got Aaron to hire us a couple; one was a young girl that I taught to cook and clean and wash and iron and generally do everything that I figured a wife should be doing; the other was a big strapping fellow who would drive me into town in our new surrey whenever I wanted to go, and he would get the firewood and fetch water and do any heavy lifting needed around the house.

Once I got them trained, Aaron was happy as a pup, because his home was always clean and neat, his meals were always on time, the fire was always laid, and he had this cute young wife to show off whenever we went to town. I've never felt bad about how I treated him or all the things I got him to do for me; I feel certain that I gave him eleven of the best years of his life. My life with Aaron was the best it had ever been, too, but that's not to say, I was sorry to see him go.

Now, here I was, twenty-eight years old, I owned a well-run farm, I had good farm-hands and good domestics, I had learned to play the piano – or at least a few songs – and I felt like my own life was just beginning. What I wanted to do now was pretty much up to me, and for the next two years, I didn't do anything much but shop from the catalogues for nice clothes and begin to take advantage of being "the widow Dalton" in as many of the social circles I could find in our little country town and the neighborhood. But I did start shopping, more or less on the sly, for one other item that I knew I would eventually want: a real man who would care only for me.

Morgan Orbison, who owned the Savings and Loan, had only one son, Paul, and a couple of very plain-looking daughters. When I offered to help the older one, Mabel, with her wardrobe and make-up, I pretty much had a key to their front door and won a glowing introduction to the son. Paul Orbison was a bit on the dumpy side, but very well-spoken and quite pleasant in his genteel advances, and his financial future was rosier than any farmer's and a lot less dusty.

Calvin Douglas was a big, German man who owned the land next to mine and had just turned his farm into a ranch to raise a sort of new breed of horse he said was a Tennessee Walking Horse. I didn't know much about them, but they were beautiful and apparently had some lovely gait that made them a special breed. He had never been married, as far as anyone knew, and he was a few years older than me, but he was an extraordinarily good-looking man, and this new horse breed of his might really turn out to be something for the future. Before Aaron died, we had been to a barn-raising and a couple of dances at his place, and he was not only extremely courteous and attentive to me, but also a fine dancer.

The only other male in the whole county who wasn't poor, married, too young or too old was Jeremiah Brown, who sold a lot of the best mules around and, if you cleaned him up a bit, maybe wasn't too bad looking. I wasn't too sure if he could ever get rid of the smell, but I thought I'd give him a quick try before I started concentrating on the other two.

I invited all three to the barn dance but spent most of my time with Jeremiah to see if the other two had enough interest to be jealous. I may have miscalculated, because Louisa Guthrie was sort of allover Calvin from the get-go, and she's about five or six years younger than me, was never married, and is so "bubbly" she almost makes me throw up; she didn't seem to affect Calvin in that way at all, as far as I could tell; the big oaf. Paul made a few gentle efforts to shake me loose from Jeremiah, which I encouraged, but he just seemed awful timid about the whole thing, but at least he did try.

Jeremiah turned out to be quite a pleasant surprise. He may have had to take a bath in lye or something, but the mule odor was all gone, and with a trimmer beard, he was not bad looking at all. While no great shakes on the dance floor, I couldn't have hired a more thoughtful beaux out of a gigolo service; he was constantly getting me punch or finding a chair for me or fanning me with his hat. I decided that night that he was a nice safe place to fall back on if Paul wouldn't take the right steps

So the next two months I spent working on Paul and dropping hints; I had him over for supper almost every Sunday evening and even invited the ugly sisters a couple of times, and it was all nice and charming and "homey," but he didn't seem to be responding, so I thought maybe I'd get Jeremiah back in the mix and see if that might light a fire under my very conservative banker's son The next Sunday I invited Jeremiah over for supper.

He was all scrubbed down, with no trace of the mules, even though he had ridden over on one. Why did he do that, he's got two or three nice mares? I played the piano for him, which he thought was almost magic, and then I sat right next to him on the settee instead of in my chair, and took his hand. I started telling him how lonely it was not to have a man around the house, and that some nights I was downright frightened, being all by myself. I had told Paul pretty much the same stuff, but a lot more subtly. When it was time for him to go, I kissed him on the cheek and pressed up against him for a few seconds; I don't think he's likely to forget that.

Over the next few days, I was surprised at how often I found myself thinking of Jeremiah. I just couldn't stop thinking how much fun it would be to have him around and be able to get him to do almost anything I wanted; and he was really kind of good looking in a rough sort of way and, of course, he was strong as an ox . . . or in his case, as a mule, and was certainly used to a hard day's work. Maybe Jeremiah was good for something better than just bait. So, I decided to give my reluctant banker one more try, and if he didn't show a little more gumption, maybe I'd take old Jeremiah and see what I could make of him.

The next Sunday, I had Paul come out for dinner. I wore that real tight dress that I got mail-order from Marshall Field's up in Chicago, and I had the girl fix creamed lima beans, which I knew he was crazy about. It went well I thought: I got him to sing along when I played "Abide with Me" and when I sat next to him on the settee and let my hand drift over onto his thigh, he just put his hand on top of mine. I did everything except come right out and ask him to ask me to marry him, and as he was taking his leave, I leaned in and kissed him on the lips, real quickly, like I couldn't help myself; and then I acted all embarrassed and I think I even managed to blush. He was embarrassed, too, but I could tell he liked that little kiss a lot. So, now, I figured I'd just wait and see which one of them was ready to do what.

Life can sure chase you down some paths you never thought you'd be on, can't it? Here I am, near four years to the day later, right back in that same hospital as before, for a reason I couldn't even have guessed at back then. Today it's all good news and celebrating, and then it seemed like the worst thing that could ever have happened to me. Just a couple a hours ago, Sue Ann gave birth to our seven-and-a-half-pound boy, Joshua, and they both are doing fine as they could be. But four years ago, Calvin Douglas hauled me in here on the back of his rig with a bunch of cracked ribs and a big knot on the back of my head, and I never got to Abbie Duncan's house at all.

Well, it kind of started when Miss Abbie asked me to her barn dance and spent almost all her time with me, even though I know I'm a pretty lame dancer. Then a couple weeks later, she asked me over to supper, and I just couldn't believe how friendly she was, and she really sounded like she needed someone to take care of her. I couldn't believe, at first, that she would even consider that person to be me, but as I was leaving, she even kissed me on the cheek, and then she must have tripped a bit or something, 'cause she fell right up against me and – I'm not making this up – she stayed there for a bit before she pushed herself away. Now that really surprised me; it was like she didn't mind being that close to me.

I had a lot to think about ... a lot to puzzle out. First of all, Miss Abbie could have her pick of any man in the county, or as far as I knew, any man in the state, so how come she was so nice to me unless she really wanted me to be the fella who would care for her. I found myself talking to my mule, Gus, a lot more than I ever done before; I mean, who else was I going to talk to about something like that? Reverend Brandywine? Not hardly. But after a while it just seemed that no matter how unlikely it might be, or how ashamed I would feel if I was wrong, if I was right, this could be the best thing that ever happened to me. I decided I would ride over to Miss Abbie's farm and ask her if she would consider marrying me and letting me look out for her. So, the next Sunday, I gave Gus and me a good cleaning up, hiked up on his back, and off we went.

We just made the turn in the road where we could see Miss Abbie's house up ahead, and I remember saying to Gus, "There's where your new mistress lives, Gus," and he stopped dead as a post. I didn't have no idea what was wrong, but I figured he must a seen a snake or something, so I got down and looked all around but couldn't see nothing that should have spooked him, so I thought I'd just walk with him for a spell and took hold of the reins, but he wouldn't budge. I gave him a couple of good tugs, but he had his front feet firmly planted, and he didn't want to move. I never had occasion to put the whip to Gus because he had always just done what I told him without no fuss, so I was in a bit of pickle here; I didn't want to go get a branch and hit him, but I sure wasn't going to stand in the middle of the road arguing with no mule. But that's when I made a little mistake — I stepped back and slapped him on his rear haunch with my hand; there was a blur and some dead serious pain in my chest and the next thing I remember was laying in the back of Calvin Douglas' rig and a couple a guys in white coats unloading me onto some kind a stretcher.

I spent near a week in here because one of the doctors was worried about whether one of those broken ribs had punched a little hole in my lung; turned out it didn't, but that wasn't nowhere near the best news. The best news was that Sue Ann Crowley was the nurse who was taking care of me and a more perfect "angel of mercy" you couldn't a dreamed up. Not only was she sweet and gentle, but when she heard that I bred mules, she wanted to know all about it; she was a city girl who went to nursing school in Chattanooga and had just moved out here a couple of months ago to find hospital work, and all this country stuff was brand new to her.

Over the next couple of months after they let me out, Sue Ann and me spent as many of her off hours together as was seemly, and many the evening she would have to push me out the front door of her rooming house, 'cause I never really wanted to leave her. She would come out to the farm when she had a whole day off, and we would take rides around the county and have picnics and go to barn dances and church socials and the like, and often she would cook dinner at my farm. I never had no idea that country life was so different from city life, but Sue Ann just thought this kind of living was the best thing on earth. Somehow or another, Miss Abbie just got kicked out of my mind, until someone told me that she and banker Orbison's son was getting married. Maybe that's what prompted me, but I know I would a done it sooner or later, so I asked Sue Ann to marry me and, there we were at a nurses' station in the hospital, and she just threw her arms around my neck and kissed me plum on the mouth, in front of God and everybody! Sue Ann is like that – always full of surprises.

We went over to her home in Chattanooga to get married, so I met her mother and father and older brother. Both of the men was in the Union army, but nobody seemed to talk much about the war anymore; we were coming up on the "millennium – the year 1900 was fast approaching, and most everybody you talked to had high hopes for this new century. I had got a real nice surrey from Cleve Newman in Oak Grove, so we drove over in that and then took our time riding through the mountains on our way home. They have a lot of real nice inns over in that part of the state and a lot of pretty impressive scenery.

It didn't take Sue Ann long to have our old farmhouse looking real warm and cozy; 'course she threw out almost everything there except the two stoves, but whatever she did was fine with me. She was still working regular shifts at the hospital until about two months ago, and she sure loves her work. I got her a neat little rig from Newman and taught her how to handle it, so she can always come and go pretty much as she pleases. Every once in a while, she tells me she has never been happier in her whole life, and although I've never been much of a fancy talker, I find myself saying that sort of thing to her, too. Life is pretty good.

As for my "accident," Gus had apparently just come on home and went in the barn after he put me in the hospital. I figured he'd be feeling pretty bad about what he done to me, but the first time I saw him after I got home, he looked me straight in the eye, nodded his head up and down and kinda smiled, like it was just something that had to be done. I had to ponder on that for a while, but I finally figgered maybe Gus saw something dangerous down the road and felt like he had to do something. Well, it cost me a couple a broken ribs, but considering how good everything turned out, I couldn't really argue with that. Like I said, some mules are a lot smarter than some people … and sometimes that includes me.

21

The End

HANSON'S DAUGHTER

Hanson's daughter. That's all anyone ever called her. Of course, she had a front name, but somehow it was seldom used. Just – Hanson's daughter. She hadn't come down from that big old house on the hill for over three years. She had Maude to cook and clean for her and Boyd Clinton to take care of the house and yard, so you could look at it like she just didn't need to come into town. Still it was strange, and that was probably why even though she was out of sight she was not out of mind. Somebody would tell her story every time a stranger sat down long enough to listen.

The last time she was seen by anyone in town was when Boyd drove her down in the buckboard with old Hanson's body in the back. That was a Saturday, and it was raining; everybody who remembers anything about that day remembers it was raining. That morning, Boyd rode down to the Sheriff's office and told him that old man Hanson was dead. Sheriff Newton got the Coroner, who was Delbert White at the time, and they went up to the house and found old Hanson sitting at his desk with a good-sized hole in the right side of his head and a Colt .45 on the floor next to him. There was a note saying, "I'm sorry" and signed in full, "Hiram J. Hanson." The Sheriff and the Coroner followed Boyd and the girl to J. J. Johnson's Funeral Parlor, and she tried to make arrangements to have him buried the next day. We don't generally have funerals on a Sunday around here, but Jonah Johnson, J. J.'s oldest son, said the girl was shaking like a leaf and seemed so near collapse that he gave into her and worked into the night to get old Hanson ready for burial. The girl slept that night at the Funeral Home; she in the Parlor and Boyd on the porch. It was still raining.

The next morning it had stopped raining. Jonah and a helper loaded Hanson's coffin onto the buckboard, and they all went to the cemetery where the two grave-diggers had just finished. Sheriff Newton, a deputy, the two grave-diggers, Jonah and his helper, and Hanson's daughter were the only ones in attendance. As soon as she threw a handful of dirt on the coffin, she got up on the buckboard and waited until Boyd drove her home. We know this to be accurate because Mamie Thrasher had followed them at a discrete distance and posted herself on the crest of Sherman's Hill where she could see everything. It's not hard to believe that Mamie was there because she was widely accepted as the nosiest woman in West Tennessee.

Hanson's Bank didn't open that Monday, because nobody was quite sure what to do, but Tuesday a couple of people went to the Mayor and told him they needed to do business there, so he rode up the hill and came down with a set of keys and got in touch with the four bank employees and got them to come in to work. The Bank kind of ran itself for a couple of weeks, with Clara Fink, Hanson's secretary, sort of directing traffic . . . until Lyle Compton rode into town. He got a room at the Strand Hotel, showed the bank employees a letter signed by

Hanson's daughter appointing him the new Manager, and settled in to run Hanson's Building & Loan.

Old Hanson was a tough man to borrow money from, but he was the only one around with money to lend, so we dealt with him and made do. It turned out that Lyle Compton was an easy-going man, who was a good listener and was willing to take the chance that most folks were too embarrassed or too religious, to cheat. He soon was accepted as an all-around fine fellow – except for one little thing. Every Friday evening, when he locked up, he took a bag with the week's deposits and rode up the hill to see Hanson's daughter – and he didn't come back until about noon on Saturday. So, you can get a good idea why Hanson's daughter is often a topic of conversation around town.

About two years ago, Lyle married the youngest Wiggins girl, and everyone figured that would be the end of his trips up the hill – but everyone was wrong. His bride seemed perfectly satisfied with the arrangement and told anyone who was brazen enough to ask that Lyle and Hanson's daughter had a lot of banking business to deal with, and they often worked late into the night. She thought that it was nice that the girl put him up in the guest room and saw that he had breakfast in the morning. The Wiggins girl may not be much brighter than a barrel of hammers, but if she wasn't concerned, what business was it of ours? We could think whatever we wanted.

Charlotte Hanson was just a few weeks older than eleven when her mother died, and she missed her a lot. She was thirteen years, two months, and seven days old when her father came into her bedroom one night and held her in his arms and comforted her and kissed her gently. That was a Wednesday. She was glad of the comforting because she still missed her mother very much. The next night he came in again and held her and comforted her and kissed her gently on the lips. Every Friday evening since then he had come in and held her and comforted her and kissed her … and entered her. She snuggled in his arms through the night. It only hurt, at first, and even though she liked the tenderness and the attention, she wondered if there might be something wrong about all this. Her father was always very kind to her, and she couldn't remember ever really wanting anything that he didn't get for her, so she shrugged it off.

He bought her a gentle roan mare, and they would often go riding together on Saturdays, although never toward town, always into the hills or along the river. Every other month or so, Boyd would drive them down to Memphis in the surrey, and Old Hanson would buy her new dresses and new shoes and things. One time, he bought her a string of pearls, which became her favorite possession.

When she was in her third year of high school, she met this boy that she liked a lot, and she told her father about him. He seemed pleased that she had found a friend her own age. He was very strict about her coming straight home from school and not going out at night, so she hadn't made any close friends. A couple of weeks later her father told her that he wasn't sure this boy could be trusted because a friend told him that this boy beat his horse something awful. He wondered if she really wanted to go on being friends with someone like that, and since she surely didn't, she stopped seeing him. After that, somehow, she became a little suspicious of all the boys at school, and she began to wonder if she would ever find someone her age who would love her like her father did.

At the beginning of her senior year, she overheard a couple of her male classmates talking about going away to college; something that she had never heard of before. When she asked her father about it, he told her that college was mostly for men because they had to go into business. She shouldn't worry herself about that because she would always live here and be taken care of. They could even take a trip as far as Nashville if she really wanted to get away from Atoka for a while. Her father loved her, and he always knew best. Still, she had this nagging feeling that, although she was very satisfied with her life right now, there was something (or someone) out there that called to her.

It was while she was reading this book about a young girl who had a pen pal that the idea first occurred to her. Since she was going to spend the rest of her life in this town, that was no reason not to make friends with people who were far away and could tell her about the world beyond. The first people she thought of were the sales girls and the clerks in Memphis, but she realized she didn't really know any of their last names. She was anxious to take their next shopping trip.

"Fate" or "Chance" or something, presented her with another opportunity while she was sitting at her father's desk one afternoon after school. Right on top, next to where she put her books down, was a letter from Lyle Compton, the Assistant Manager of the First Farmer's Bank of Memphis, inquiring about a job. She picked it up and read it. He told all about his experience and how interested he was in a position in a Savings & Loan. Her father had written "Clara, tell him not now," across the bottom of the letter. Clara was his secretary at the Bank. Charlotte thought: "What if I write to him, tell him I'm Hanson's daughter and suggest that maybe I could talk to my father if he would tell me more about himself?" That way, they could start writing to each other, and maybe she *could* talk to her father somewhere down the line, and meanwhile she would have a "pen pal." Maybe she could even figure out how to meet him on one of their trips to Memphis.

Lyle Compton was quite eager to keep up correspondence with this bright young girl whose father owned a Savings & Loan. They wrote often, sometimes twice a week, for the next few months, telling each other about their daily lives, their likes, and dislikes and eventually confessing very shyly that they each had feelings for the other. They still hadn't met, but Charlotte was positive her father would take her to Memphis for her graduation present, and she told Lyle to meet her in the shoe department at Goldsmith's at three p.m. on the Saturday after graduation. Her father always stayed with her to see that the dresses she picked out were modest, but he usually left her to buy her own shoes while he sat in a bar just across the street and waited for her. The day came, and Charlotte and her father headed for Memphis and a new chapter in her life.

It was two-fifteen when they got to Goldsmith's, and she had hurriedly decided on two dresses after her father insisted than one was not enough. She kissed him good-bye, and walked, with heart-pounding anticipation to the Shoe Department. Lyle Compton was a very trim twenty-two-year-old, sandy-haired gentleman about the same height as her father, with the two warmest brown eyes Charlotte had ever seen. Her heart had been pounding, and it now stopped altogether! When he reached out and took her hand, her knees could barely support her, and when he grabbed her around the waist to keep her from falling, she gave herself up and folded into his arms. Something similar and equally unusual must have overtaken him because he held her close and kissed her full on the mouth – a spectacle unseen before, and probably since, in Goldsmith's Shoe Department, and certainly not in 1891.

They escaped from the shocked stares around them and found a bench in the central lobby where they sat, holding hands, and tried with only modest success to explain their inexplicable behavior. "He must see her again; he could never let her go;" – "she had never known happiness before, she would never leave him." Yes, yes, of course – but how was all this to be accomplished? Lyle's plan was to meet her father and formally request her hand in marriage; if there were a place for him at the Saving & Loan he would move to Atoka; if not, they would set up housekeeping in Memphis. Charlotte may have been a bit light-headed at the moment, but she sensed that the direct route might not be the best path – all things considered. The "things" in this case, was her relationship with her father; still hard for her to understand and way too complex to explain to Lyle, so she told him to be patient and she would handle it. Their farewell kiss that Saturday was filled with promise and a newly purposed Charlotte crossed the street to open a lengthy and life-changing dialogue with her father.

Barely a week later, she told him that she was corresponding with this young man who was also in the banking business and that she really wanted to go to Memphis and meet him. She would take Maude with her to avoid any impropriety. Again, Hanson seemed delighted that she had met someone she liked, but the idea of meeting him in Memphis was out of the question for any eighteen-year-old girl of good family. Certainly, no stranger was going to be invited to come here before a serious investigation of his character was made; that would take time. She wrote to Lyle that her father was very conservative and that it would take a bit more time before they could move forward with their plans. Lyle was willing to come at any time and face her father, but she advised him to be patient because her father really had her best interests at heart, and she knew, in time, he would eventually give in to her wishes. When "time" stretched into the second month, Charlotte sensed that she had to confront her father and explain what had happened. She told him that she was in love with Lyle Compton and that he wanted to marry her.

She had really never seen her father angry before, and he was far more violent than she had ever thought him capable. He told her that he had given her *everything;* he loved her more than anyone ever could and that she would *never* leave him. He locked her in her room on a Tuesday, sent Maude to bring her meals, and didn't come into her room until Friday night when he took her by force and locked her in again.

By the following Monday, Charlotte knew she would have to ask his forgiveness if she was ever to get out of her room. She wrote a long note, apologizing and telling him she was a stupid, silly girl for not appreciating all he had done for her and recognizing how much his love meant to her.

He let her out the next Thursday evening. They both told each other how sorry they were, how much they really loved each other, and how they would try to put all this behind them. They slept together in her bed that night, and he stayed home from the Bank Friday so they could go riding in the afternoon. That evening after dinner, her father sat her on the living room sofa and put a diamond ring on her ring finger; it was his mother's, and he wanted her to wear it and stay with him always. They slept together again that night, and the next morning, she shot him in the head.

Last Saturday morning Boyd rode down the hill to Sheriff Newton's office and told him that Lyle Compton was dead. The Sheriff got the Coroner, who was now Silas Stark, and they went up to the house and found Lyle slumped in old Hanson's desk chair with a good-sized hole in the right side of his head and that old Colt .45 on the floor next to him. There was a note saying "I'm sorry, I can't go on like this" and signed "Lyle." Boyd and the Coroner loaded the body on the buckboard and brought it down to Johnson & Sons Funeral Parlor. Hanson's daughter didn't come down the hill this time. Again, it rained most of the day. He was buried last Wednesday, and there was a nice turnout for the Wake at Ellen's Diner on Maple Street, sponsored by the Savings and Loan. Hanson's daughter didn't come down for that either. At the Wake, Sheriff Newton asked me if I remembered whether Lyle was right or left-handed, and I told him "right-handed" – the last left-handed person who got a haircut from me was old Hiram Hanson. Most people run a comb through their hair after, and I always notice which hand they use.

That reminded the Sheriff that old Hanson also had a bullet in the *right* side of his head. The next morning, he rode up the hill to have a chat with Hanson's daughter, but she was out riding. She wasn't back that evening because he sent a deputy to check on her. The next morning when he went up, she was still gone; "She rode off," Boyd said, "towards Memphis, and she left these." He gave the Sheriff two envelopes: one, turned the Bank over to the four employees, and the other deeded her home to Maude and Boyd Clinton. Boyd was the last one ever to see her.

Sheriff Newton is a practical man. He had no proof that old man Hanson was murdered and even less that Lyle Compton might have been. He figured he didn't have much chance of finding a young woman, with a two-day head start and with who knows how many weeks of bank deposits in her purse, if she didn't want to be found. Not in a city as big as Memphis. There were over a hundred thousand people living there if you can believe it.

After all, he couldn't actually prove old man Hanson *wasn't* a suicide, and besides … who knew anything, really, about what life might have been like up there on that hill … for Hanson's daughter.

THE END

Ginger

I took clarinet lessons for a couple of years in grade school, so when I got to high school, I was pretty excited when they put me in the band. That way I got to go to all the basketball games and, more importantly at the time, football games. Because that meant that I *had* to be out on a lot of Friday nights. The other neat thing was that I got to be around a lot of upper-classmen; not that they would talk to me, but at least I got to listen to them and find out what was *really* going on. One of the guys, Frank Brooks, was a sophomore and the same age as me, but he played on the first clarinet stand, and I was on the fourth. He had his own dance band, and he would talk to me once in a while. He was the one who told me if I was ever interested in being in a dance band, I should learn the saxophone. I started pestering Ma about it because she was the one who made me learn the clarinet.

I had been sacking at the A & P after school, and during the summer, so I had a little saved up for a car when I hit sixteen, but as soon as I heard about the possibility of playing in a dance-band I changed my mind on the spot. The way it worked out was, I told the bandmaster that I wanted to learn the saxophone, but when he asked which one, I had no idea. So, he said, "Well, there's an old tenor in the band-room that some kid left here a couple of years ago. If you pay for new pads and a tune-up, and can come up with forty dollars, I'll let you have it." Sounded great to me, 'cause I knew I could eventually get Ma to wheedle the money for lessons out of Pa. And that's how I started playing the tenor sax.

The freshman classroom was in a little wooden building between the regular high school and the gym, and by November, we could all tell that there was no real heat in that shack. There was some kind of big contraption hanging in the back of the room that was supposed to be a "space heater," but it never came close to warming the space that was our classroom. So that was another great thing about being in the band, and also about taking lessons on the sax: I could always go to the gym where it was nice and warm because that's where the band rehearsed; I could even go there during lunch when most of us freshmen had to stay in the yard or go back into that freezing classroom. I guess I probably did practice a lot more than I would have because I went in there and picked up the tenor almost every lunch hour from November into April.

I worked at the A & P that summer, again, and had to start all over saving for the car, because paying for the sax took me back down to practically nothing. I did practice some during the summer, and I felt like I could probably play the sax as well or better than I played the clarinet; I think it's an easier horn. Boy, I was really glad I did, because when I went back to band practice, the week before school started, the bandmaster, Mr. Edwards, asked me if I'd like to try to play the baritone sax. The guy who played it the last four years in the concert band graduated, and left it behind, and Mr. Edwards wanted someone to replace him. So now I was also in the concert band as well as the marching band; clarinet in one and baritone sax in the other. And I got to use the baritone without having to pay for it. That was really neat.

Frank Brooks was also in the concert band and also first stand, so I saw a lot more of him now, and he thought my being able to handle the baritone as well as the tenor was really smooth. His dance band played at one of the YMCA dances, so I went to hear them; they were really good. What was a big surprise was that they had this girl singer with them who had a terrific voice and was so cute you'd think she should be in the movies or something. It turned out she was Frank's older sister, even though she was just a little thing. Her name was Ginger, and I asked her if that was because of the color of her hair and she sternly corrected me, "No, that's my name. And my hair is auburn." So, I figured I was not off to a very good start with her. I went to a lot of dances that Frank played that year, at least the ones that were free; I didn't try talking to Ginger very much, because I realized I didn't have much to say to her other than that I thought she was the prettiest girl in the world. It looked like our first conversation might also be our last.

Frank and I were getting along real good, and two of the guys in his band were in my class, Corky Rable, who was his second trumpet, and "Red" Orbinson, who played drums. Of course, both of them were in the school band, so I got to know them a lot better during that school year. When June came around, Frank found out his fourth tenor was going off to college so he asked me if I'd like to come sit in on a couple of rehearsals to see "if I liked playing in a dance band," but I think it was more to see if I could cut the charts they used with both the tenor and the baritone. I guess it turned out that I could because Frank asked me to join them for a gig on Labor Day at the Boat Club. I've never kidded myself – next to Frank and some of the guys in his band I was never anything more than a journeyman musician.

The past week we had just rehearsed Stan Kenton's charts for "Opus in Pastels" with me playing the baritone, and when we closed the next to last set with it, the crowd liked it a lot. That was really a kick because that orchestration was as difficult as anything I'd ever read. Also, a lot of the guys in the band slapped me on the back at the end of the night and said, "Okay" or "Good Job" or something like that, and Ginger said, "I'm glad you're joining us … that was a great sound tonight." I was pretty much walking on air after that, even though she took off with Bobby Prescott, the lead trumpet before I could even say thank you.

But I never forgot what a lucky thing it was that the only sax that was available for me to learn was a tenor; if it had been an alto, Frank would probably have never had a place for me to join the band. I've always felt that meeting Frank Brooks was one of the best things that ever happened to me. The regular guys in the band didn't want to rehearse much, so I was a little worried about all this new music that I was practically sight-reading; they had been playing most of these tunes for months and months, and they only wanted to rehearse when they got new charts. I asked Frank if I could take my charts home and practice some, and he said, "Sure, just give Ginger a call, she manages the band and takes care of all that stuff."

Ginger was two years older than Frank and me, and she had her own apartment over on the East side and worked at the Farmers Insurance office. I called her and told her what I wanted, and she said to come on over, the next night, any time after six. I rang the bell when I got to her place about six-thirty and waited a while, but nothing happened, so I figured maybe she wasn't home yet. I thought I'd knock real hard on the door, and if that didn't get an answer, then she must not be home for sure. I knocked, and then I heard her call from inside, "Come in," so I opened the door and stepped inside. That was a mistake. She was standing in the middle of the room, holding a towel in front of her; her hair was wet, and she was mad as the dickens.

"What the hell do you think you're doing, Wally?"

"I'm sorry, Ginger … you said to come in."

"I did not say for you to come in!"

"I'm really sorry, Ginger … but you said it twice."

"No, you clown – I said, 'I'm coming, I'm coming.'"

"Oh, Ginger … I'm really …"

"You think I would ask you to come in when I'm standing here half-naked?"

"No, Ginger … I'm sure …"

"Well, for crying out loud, TURN AROUND, Wally … and quit staring at me!"

(I did) "I'm really sorry, Ginger …"

"Well, you ought to be … coming into a woman's apartment …"

"But see, Ginger, I thought sure you said …"

"And DON'T turn around." (I had turned a bit.)

"Sorry." (I turned back.)

"Yeah, right."

"… and I didn't mean to be staring …"

"Well, you were."

"Sorry."

"All right … all right … just stay there while I get a robe on."

"Sure, Ginger ... I won't move."

"You better not."

"I won't, Ginger ... it's just that I was sure I heard ..."

"Then clean out your damn ears, Wally."

"Yes'm ... (door slam) ... sorry."

So, that didn't go too well, either.

While I was waiting ... I didn't want to turn around too much, but what I could see was mostly a nice neat room with light tan walls and a couple of bookcases jammed with orchestration charts, and two file cabinets with a door sitting on top to make a desk. When she came back, and I was allowed to move, I could see a little kitchenette and a door off to the right that must have been the bedroom, and another door that I guess was the bathroom, and a small table with two chairs, and a big sofa with a lot of pillows and one sort of overstuffed chair opposite it, with a coffee table in between, and a super-looking record changer with a pile of 45's and 78's stacked all around it. I hadn't noticed it before, but she had a Dorsey record on real low, and they were playing "Marie." I guess I'm telling you this because I was so nervous; I don't know what to say about Ginger.

She had on some kind of oriental thing, maybe what you would call a kimono, but it only came down to just above her knees; it was trimmed in black with a lot of red and green and black dragon-like things all over it, and it was tied with a big black sash. Her hair was almost dry, but she was still toweling it and then sort of combing it with her fingers; she was wearing ballet shoes, and she looked so tiny and vulnerable that I could hardly stand it. She was all business now and told me where to start looking for the tenor and baritone charts. She said she had to fix dinner, so she went to that kitchen area and told me to ask her whenever I needed help. Well, it turned out that I needed her help pretty soon because I really didn't know what all the band used as standards, so we were pretty close to each other while she was pulling charts and showing me where stuff was. Darn … she smelled so … like a flower.

She did most of the talking; I was afraid to say anything. She had pretty much forgotten about fixing dinner, and I think she must have also forgotten about me being such an idiot because she was so concerned about wanting me to get everything I would need. It took us close to a half-hour before she said, "Okay, I think that's it," and then I just stood there looking at her when I heard the record changer drop a new record on the turntable and Artie Shaw's band started playing "Stardust."

"Damn."

"What's the matter, Ginger, did I …

"No, Wally, it's not you … it's just me."

"Oh! Are you okay?"

"It's just this darn song and this arrangement."

"Oh … *'Stardust',* huh?"

"Yeah … the lyrics are so sad … and that trumpet solo just kills me."

"Well, our band plays his chart, don't we?

"Don't I know it."

"… and you don't like it?"

"No, I love it … I love it … but it makes me all … funny inside."

"Oh … and we play it almost every gig …"

"Yeah, and I have to sit there and smile … while I'm trying not to jump off the bandstand and grab some stranger and make him dance with me."

"Oh, gee … that must be … weird … I'm so sorry …"

"No … it's just that song … that arrangement … how can you *not* want to have someone holding you?"

"Yeah, I guess … does Frank know? Maybe he …"

"He knows, but you can't play a dance without somebody requesting it."

"No … that's for sure."

"That's just the way it goes."

"Yeah … but …"

"Hey … it's *my* problem"

"Well, yes … but …"

"That's why I play it once in a while … trying to get over it."

"… well … I wish there was something I could do?"

"Yeah, right … (a long pause) … no, wait a minute!"

"What …?"

"It's half over … dance with me."

"… uh … what?"

"You can slow dance, can't you, Wally?"

"Well, yes … but …"

"No buts, Wally … just put your arms around me and don't talk."

"Oh, gee, Ginger … I …"

"Shut up, Wally … just be quiet and dance."

She put my arms around her waist and put her arms around my neck and when she leaned into me … I thought … no, I have no idea what I thought ... I have no idea what I felt ... all I can tell you is ... even to this day ... I've never experienced anything more ... amazing ... more wonderful ... than that minute or so, holding her until "Stardust" played out.

When it was over, she stepped back and held both my hands and said, "Thanks, Wally – that was really nice ... go home now." I don't remember saying anything; I don't think I could have. I went home.

I don't know ... sometimes I really do believe that the whole world is divided into musicians and laymen ... at least as far as guys are concerned ... I mean, with musicians, at least there is something inside of them that is a sort of ... I don't know ... sensitive? ... or maybe just a soft spot, or something like that ... oh, yeah, a lot of them are all absorbed in their music, but it seems like most of them can treat you like you're not just a piece of meat ... I mean the guys in the office are always grabbing and making ugly jokes and like, leering at you ... and that's supposed to be attractive? ... and if you do go out with one of them, they think dinner and a movie is their ticket to ride ... and they're all pissed if you don't drop your drawers on the first date like that's what they paid for ... but musicians, at least, you can go out with them, and maybe even fool around a little, but if you tell 'em that's it, they back off ... well almost all the time ... if you make it real clear ... and I know they probably smoke too much weed, but generally that makes them a little easier to talk down ... and besides, I can understand why they smoke because I like to take a hit or two before we start the set, 'cause it just sort of loosens you up, and you feel relaxed about doing your thing ... but I don't need it on a regular basis ... and the ones who snort or go to the needle, you can always tell just by looking at their eyes, so you just don't even get close to them ... I think I could probably handle them, but I figure they are headed towards a place where I don't want to be ... I mean how the hell do they think they're going to survive in the real world ... the real world is tough, and you got to watch your back at all times ... Frank and I know that, we've seen it all our lives ... we've got two younger brothers and a younger sister, and we know damn well that Mom and Pop have to work their asses off just to keep this family above water ... life without money is no life at all ... it's just drudgery ... and that's not the life for me ... so that's why it's so hard for me to find somebody ... the nice ones, the ones I could like, almost all seem to be musicians, and I can't see how any of them are ever going to get by on that unless they go over to Nashville and break into the Country scene there ... and don't tell me that's not a long-shot ... and the office types that I've met just seem like real goons ... like Neanderthals or something ...with nothing to offer, except the possibility of making a decent living ... yeah, I need to find someone like my brother ... Frank's a sweetheart ... he likes absolutely everybody, and nothing seems to get him down, and here he is working at that Paper company during the day and taking night classes to get a college degree, and he's still a heck of a musician along with all that ... and Gordon was okay, but he doesn't seem to have much ambition, even though he plays a great horn ... and he's also a sloppy kisser ... I could take only so much of that ... Bobby is working on the line at the Ford plant, but he really isn't much interested in anything but playing music, so I can't tell where his head is at ... and the two guys at work that I dated for a while don't know squat about music, and don't even care that I'm a band singer ... hey, pay attention, I got a life, too, you know ... and why should it be so hard to find a guy who thinks of me before he thinks of himself ... is there nobody out there?... well, okay, not counting Wally ... he's more like a cocker spaniel ... with those big soulful brown eyes... and, yeah, those ears ... not that they're as big as a spaniel's, but they are big ...and they stick out like two jug handles ... no, that's not fair, they're not that bad ... and he is sweet ... sweet as can be ... and I can see it in his eyes — I can do no wrong as

---

I played in Frank's band all through my junior and senior year and the summer between and the summer after I graduated. Ginger would always say, "Hey, Wally," and I would always say, "Hey, Ginger;" and when Frank called up "Stardust," I looked at her, and she turned and smiled at me, but that was about it. She had quit dating our trumpet player, and then dated Gordon Turbridge, (trombone), for a little while. I dated or at least went out with four or five girls, but none of them very long. Made out a little, here and there, but never went all the way, but – I got to admit, I'm kind of goofy looking, so I'm pretty grateful when a girl even lets me kiss her. Besides, there was no one I really wanted to be with except Ginger, even though I knew darn well that was a pipedream.

In September, I went up to Austin Peay College in Clarksville because they were a good school for teachers, and that's what I wanted to be, and I got a partial scholarship. It's about forty miles north of Nashville, so it only takes me less than three hours to drive there. Yeah, I finally got a car; it's a '47 blue Chevy coupe, so it's got a few miles on it, but it hadn't been in any wrecks, and Mom and Pop gave me a hundred dollars for graduation which meant I had enough to get *something*. I'd had to dip into the old savings again because Mr. Edwards wouldn't let me use the baritone now that I was out of school, so I had to buy it, and it was expensive, but as long as Frank was going to keep me in the band, it was worth every penny.

The way it worked was, Frank found another fourth tenor to fill in during the week because I couldn't come home for a gig unless it was on a Friday or Saturday night. Fortunately for me, many of the weekend gigs were for better money, and he could add the baritone; so, when he could use me, I would drive down Friday afternoon or Saturday morning and head back to school Sunday afternoon; it was great. I got in the college band, too; I think it was because they hadn't been using a baritone sax, so I was kind of a novelty.

There was nothing that I liked as much as playing in Frank's band, and I would go to any lengths to keep being a part of it. I have to admit that the chance just to see Ginger every couple of weeks was a pretty strong motivation. I almost didn't want to go away to college because I would miss her so much, and I foolishly hoped that if I were around, at least she wouldn't get serious with anybody else. Stupid! Sure enough, during my first semester at Austin Peay, she hooked up with some guy, and before the school year was over, she was married. They just got married at the Justice of the Peace; no big fancy wedding or anything.

During that summer, I was able to get a couple of days at the A & P, sacking, but the neat thing was that I got a part-time job as a teacher's assistant at Putnam High School down on Jackson Street. I graded test papers and generally ran errands for Mr. Whitcome, who was teaching remedial English in the summer school. So, between the two, and some pretty regular band gigs, I did okay that summer, at least, money-wise. Not so good in the rest of my life, which pretty much centered around Ginger.

The good-news-bad-news was that Ginger seemed really happy; of course, I wanted her to be … but you know. The guy, Chet Coughlin, was really good looking, and even worse, everybody in the band seemed to like him a lot. Swell! He came to a lot of the dances, not all, but a lot, and he seemed to get to know people real quick, because almost every time he came, before the evening was over, he would be dancing with two or three of the women there. I would hear Ginger teasing him about it, but they would both be laughing, so I guess it didn't really bother her.

During high school, the band would wear tuxes for the fancy dances (Ma bought me one), but if we played the Y or some high school hop, we would just be in dark pants, with a jacket and tie. That summer, Frank bought us all navy-blue vests and blue ties, and we all got navy blue slacks on our own and wore plain white shirts; it was a neat move, and we all felt pretty spiffy in our new outfits. "Blue Flame" was Frank's theme song. To go with it, Ginger got a pale blue off-the-shoulder cocktail dress, and with her figure and that auburn hair she was something to behold. I beheld her every chance I got. She also got a new black evening gown that accented her tiny waist and had a slit up the left side that was very … distracting.

My second year up in Clarksville was much like the first; studies were hard, and a couple of them were downright boring, but I knew I would finish up with my Teaching Certificate in June, so I could handle it. I came home for a week-end gig about twice a month, and Ginger and her husband seemed to be getting along just fine; they threw an anniversary party in April, I guess to make up for the fact that they didn't have much of a wedding celebration, and I came back home for that. It was hard seeing them together and Ginger being so happy, but I had to admit, Chet seemed like a heck of a nice guy, and he was always real friendly to me; I knew I was just going to have to accept this and get on with my life, but that wasn't at all easy.

When I came home in June, I had already applied to the Putnam County Board of Education for a high school teaching position; I was qualified in American History and World History, so I thought I had a pretty good chance of getting in somewhere close to town. However, nothing opened up in September, so I was still picking up a little time as an assistant at Putnam, but I really couldn't stand going back to the A & P to sack groceries. Just in the nick of time, Fred Stanton, the third alto man, got me a job driving for his father's meat market; Fred had been working in the store all through high school, and he was now a regular butcher there. It didn't pay a lot, but it saved my bacon for a while. (Get it?) It wasn't until January that I got on as a substitute, but that got my foot in the door, and then I taught History in summer school, and the following September I had my first real teaching job at the new Walt Whitman High School up in Algood.

The other thing was, Chet wasn't coming to the dances at all anymore, so sometimes Ginger would go out after a gig and have a beer with us. What was even better, she would sometimes start up a conversation with me; ask me about how I liked teaching, and what I was up to and like that. The answer, sadly, was really not much of anything. One night, when Frank and the other two guys were throwing darts, and there was just the two of us, she said, "So, tell me, Wally, have you had any luck breaking into any more apartments to get a look at naked girls?" Well, I darn near choked on my beer and had such a coughing fit she had to pound me on the back to help me recover. She couldn't keep herself from laughing out loud at me, and once I sort of got control of myself, I had to laugh, too. Every once in a while, since then, she will say, "Any luck yet, Wally?" and we both kind of grin at each other, and it feels just terrific that we have this little secret that we share. The other neat thing was, I always used to watch her when we started playing *Stardust*, and she always sat real still and sometimes would sort of fold her arms across her body, hugging herself, but a week or so after that night, she looked over at me, and I raised my eyebrows and nodded toward the dance floor, like," You want to dance?" and she just smiled this real sad smile and just nodded, "No." Man, I felt good having this kind of private communication going on with her … *real* good.

Frank was going to night school right here at Tennessee Tech, and he must have been doing well at the Paper Company because just after Christmas, he asked Dolores Hagan to marry him, and they were married that June. Dolores is not only pretty, but she is about the sweetest person you're ever going to meet; they make a great couple. Of course the whole band was there and we got to meet Ginger and Frank's parents and the three younger Brooks: Paul, who was about six-four and three years younger than Frank; Jimmy, a couple of years younger than Paul, and their little sister Martha, who was tiny like Ginger, but a real redhead, with a face full of freckles, cute as all get-out, and about ten or twelve years old.

The wedding was at the Catholic Church, I didn't know Frank was Catholic, so I guess Ginger was, too, or at least she was raised that way.

Anyway, they do a real pretty ceremony, and then we all went over to the parents' house and had a real nice cook-out, and they got one of those portable dance floors out back and, of course, Frank had a sound system and record collection that wouldn't quit, and his brother Jimmy really had a great time being the DJ. Of course, Ginger was there with Chet.

Over the last three years, I had been to a number of school things with Libby Morrison, who worked in the Principal's office up at Whitman, and she was really easy to look at, and the best thing was that she didn't mind doing most of the talking, so I never felt like there was any pressure on me to keep the ball rolling or anything. I had someone that I could take to dinner or the movies, and now, to our first dance. I liked Libby, and I guess she liked me because she always gave me a nice kiss on the lips at the end of the evening anytime we went out … so here was Ginger with her husband and me with my date, and for some reason, I felt real awkward about that … like things were out of joint, or something.

Sure enough, about two hours along, Jimmy put on Artie Shaw's *Stardust* and Libby grabbed my hand and said, "Come on, you have to dance this one with me," so we did, and there, just in the corner of the dance floor was Ginger in Chet's arms, and when they turned so I could see her face, there was a tear in the corner of her eye, and when she saw me she tried to smile but she couldn't quite make it happen. So, for no good reason, I just felt like I should be holding her … if I were holding her, she wouldn't be crying; she would know it was all right, whatever it was. But there she was, in her husband's arms, and here was me, way over here, not taking care of her at all, just holding somebody else. At that moment, I felt a part of my life was over, and there was nothing I could ever do about it.

That night when I took Libby home, she asked me to come up to her apartment, and we made love for the first time; the next morning, she told me that she was in love with me, and if I wanted, she would be very happy to marry me. I'm not sure exactly what I said then, but it must have been in line with that, because we were married a week before school started that Fall so that we would have time to go to Niagara Falls for our honeymoon.

By now, I was halfway through my fifth year of teaching American History and feeling a lot better about myself as a teacher; that first year was probably more of a learning experience for me than it was for any of my poor students. I tell you "practice teaching" and teaching real kids in a real classroom are worlds apart. I think I was just lucky to survive that first year, but now I sort of felt like I knew what I was doing and what the kids might throw at me; I don't mean literally, that still surprised me. I'd also taken a couple more history classes up at Vanderbilt during the summers and felt like I was a lot deeper into my chosen field.

Libby and I had found a real nice little house to rent out on Gibbons Road, which was only about fifteen minutes from school; Libby was as sweet as can be and seemed pretty happy all the time, and I was as happy as I guess I had any right to be. The band was sounding real relaxed and "better than ever" some folks were telling us, and Jerry Costain, the fourth tenor man, had picked up some kind of night work, so I was playing pretty much every gig on either the tenor or the baritone. So that was all good.

The only thing that sort of brought me down was that we played this New Year's Eve gig, and Ginger really seemed different. She just nodded when I said "Hey, Ginger," to her and didn't joke with me at all and didn't even look at me when we put up "Stardust."

Something was wrong.

Well, I admit … he got my attention the first time I saw him … he came into the Farmers office and said something like, "Hey, Gorgeous, I can sell anything, and I've decided I can help more people by selling them insurance than I can any other way … and if this is where you work, then I know damn well this is the place I want to be" … at first I thought he was just another big blow-hard, but he had a great resume, and he had sold more cars than anyone at Spivey Motors over in Nashville for the last four years … Spivey was the biggest Chevy dealer around — you can hear their ads all over the place … and when he wasn't trying to make an entrance or a big impression, he was really very thoughtful, and he really listened to you … which seems pretty hard for most men to do … and the guys in the office thought he was the coolest thing since sliced bread because he knew a lot about sports, about fishing, about cars, and apparently about how to attract women, because all the secretaries were darn near giddy over him … I had to admit he came in an awfully attractive package: tall, blond, muscular, a cleft in the chin and … as I found out later, very gentle hands … and he had no reservation about telling me that he thought we were meant for each other … he started talking like that the second night he took me to dinner, and it wasn't long after that I found out about his hands … and that he was more considerate of me in bed than any guy I had ever been with … a tough combination to resist … so, I held out until April, but then in bed one morning he said to me, "Babe, you know I love you. If you don't love me, then throw me back — if you love me, marry me now — today!" … so I did, not that day of course, but as soon as we could get all the legal stuff done … and it was wonderful … he moved into my place, where we had spent most of our time, and he didn't even insist on changing anything … he just dragged some more clothes over, and we bought a little dresser for him, and we rented a storage locker for all the charts, and that was it … no fuss, no mess, and we were a happily married couple … it turned out he could sell insurance just like he sold cars because his second full year with the company he booked the highest numbers of any of the salesmen except old George Graham, who literally knew everybody in town … and he sure didn't mind spending pretty much all the money he was making on us having a good time … we ate out about four or sometimes five nights a week, and … after we celebrated our anniversary, we went to New Orleans for a week and stayed in a great old hotel in the Quarter and ate at two of the best restaurants I had ever been in … One weekend we drove all the way up to Cincinnati to see the Cardinals play baseball … and we went up to Louisville to see the Derby, and I know that cost a fortune because we had seats in the Club House … yeah, we were living high on the hog, and he never stopped paying attention to anything I wanted … except, maybe, he found the band gigs a little boring after a while … and I teased him about that because when he came, he always managed to dance with three or four of the prettiest women there … but, after a while he stopped coming altogether … what I didn't know for quite a long time was that he also arranged to sleep with half of them on the nights when he didn't come … them, and I'm pretty sure, another half-dozen bored housewives, and a couple of co-eds at Tennessee Tech … yeah, he fooled me, and he was real good at it … right up to the day I found out for sure that some of those rumors I heard around the office were true, he was as gentle and as loving as ever … it was hard to take, and the thing that truly baffled me was the way he took it all in stride … when I confronted him about it, he just said how sorry he was, if he had hurt me … if? … and asked if I thought we could still go on the way we were … well, I sure as hell couldn't … I was hurt, and I didn't feel safe with him … so he just packed a bag and moved out somewhere — and came to work the next day as big as life … I couldn't take that, so I left work and went over to Frank's house and blubbered the whole sordid mess out to Dolores … she was great, she always is, and so was Frank … when he came home they both insisted that I spend a few days with them, which I did, and that helped a lot … but we had a gig on New Year's Eve, and I knew I would have to work that; Frank told me to skip it, but he didn't argue a lot when I said I wanted to do it … and the kicker was that night at the dance when Wally said, "Hey, Ginger," I thought I would just dissolve in tears on the spot … I couldn't look at him all evening because all I could think of was — how safe I felt for that one minute I was in his arms years ago …

I really had a hard time visualizing that cute little freckled-faced redhead that we met at Frank and Dolores' wedding as being old enough to get married, but there was the invitation, and in the next day's mail was a letter from Frank saying he wanted to get the old band together so we could play at his baby sister's wedding. What a great idea.

Well, a lot had happened between then and now; Frank got his degree, and shortly after, a promotion in the Paper Company sent him and Dolores to Seattle. Of course, the band broke up and most of us lost touch, but I had heard that Corky and "Red" were playing in some other band around town, and we always got our meat from Fred, so I knew there were at least a few of us who would love to play together again. I had pretty much quit music, although I would haul the clarinet out once in a while and just sit out in the backyard messing with some old song or another. Libby and I had a two-year-old son, Christopher, and Libby was now Assistant Principal. I had gone back to Austin Peay to get a better background in World History and was now teaching both, still up at Walt Whitman, and now I had tenure.

Ginger got herself transferred up to the Nashville office of Farmers, right after she divorced Chet, and I heard she married some fellow who was in the music publishing business a year or so ago. I had no idea whether she was still singing, or whether she was at all involved in the Country Music business, or even if she would be willing to come back here where she had been hurt so badly.

I got a couple of phone calls from Frank over the next few weeks, and things were looking good. He and Dolores were going to come in three days before the wedding, and he had somehow made arrangements for the band to rehearse in our old High School gym, where most of us started playing together. He didn't have any word from Ginger yet, but he had collected all the old charts and taken them with him to Seattle when Ginger left town, so we would all be reading stuff we had played a dozen, dozen times. Also, I found out he was playing in a little band up in Seattle, and he had started his own quartet; Frank was a real "music man."

Well, it was like a big reunion as we all wandered in and hugged each other and made cracks about how the "other guys" looked so old and did a certain amount of trying to catch up on almost a decade, and then Ginger walked in and everybody but Frank pretty much froze on the spot. She was absolutely gorgeous!

… No, she was stunning! That's it, stunning. Because we were all stunned. She had let her hair grow, and it framed her face and hung down her back in auburn waves almost to her waist. If her eyes were green before, they were emeralds now, and her figure was absolutely lush. She had on a dark green skirt and a simple sleeveless white blouse, and she looked as if she had just stepped off the page of some women's fashion magazine.

Frank grabbed her and swung her around and then led her over to the rest of us, who were still playing statues. When it was my turn to get a hug, I had managed to close my mouth but I'm not sure whether I was breathing yet or not. She just said, "Wally," and put her arms around my waist, and I held her for probably an inappropriate amount of time because I heard "Red" say, "Hey … it's my turn." But I did notice that she hadn't let go of me either; that was nice. While everyone was laughing, I tried counting to ten and at about seven I could feel the air coming into my lungs, so I figured I would eventually be okay.

The rehearsal went really, really well … it's amazing how that stuff comes back to you. Of course, some of the guys had never really stopped playing, but for four or five of us, this was the first time in years we had seriously sat down to play real class orchestrations of some of the absolutely great standards. Ginger sort of hummed through the six vocals that she and Frank decided on, so we never heard what she really sounded like now, all these years later, and she and Frank went off together as soon as it was over. Brother Paul was going to be the band boy for this gig, so he gathered up all the charts and equipment. So, there was no more conversation … and no more just drinking in the new Ginger.

The wedding was, again, a beautiful ceremony, but this time with a few more in the wedding party and a bit more lavish. The wedding party had their own thing after the ceremony, but all of us in the band, except Ginger and Frank went over to Dinty Moore's over on South Willow and had a couple of pitchers of draft and talked music – like in the old days. But not for long, because we all had to get home, get into tuxes and pick up the spouses and ankle out to the Boat Club for a six o'clock sit-down dinner. We were only going to play three, thirty-minute sets starting as close to eight-thirty as we could manage. Libby knew this was a pretty special night for me, so she got a new black evening gown that looked great on her, and she did look real pretty.

The dinner was very nice, and the champagne flowed like water, but all the band guys knew we had to limit that stuff or take a chance on ruining this whole affair, and nobody wanted that. All the ladies were dressed to the nines; Dolores looked great, and a couple of Martha's bridesmaids were real knock-outs in gowns that looked like they were held up by sheer willpower. Ginger's husband, I noticed, didn't come. All of us in the band excused ourselves about eight o'clock and went in the ballroom to warm up and check the mikes and sound system, and at about eight thirty-five, Frank hit the downbeat for "Blue Flame" and we were off and running.

Ginger's first vocal was "It Had To Be You," and when she finished, I thought they would never stop clapping. There was a maturity in her voice that was never there before, almost a different timbre, and when she held a note a long time and segued into the next without a breath, it could give you chills. She was better than ever – way better. We ended the first set with "One O'clock Jump" and everybody there who could find a partner was up on their feet, and most of our wives were dancing with each other. We went out back and pounded each other's backs like school kids; none of us had experienced this much sheer joy in years, even those guys who still played in other bands.

The second set was just as much fun as the first, and we closed it with "Opus in Pastels," and most of the crowd was savvy enough to appreciate what a killer piece that is, and we got a standing ovation to walk off with. We opened the final set with "Stardust," and when Frank called it up, Ginger looked over at me and raised her eyebrows and nodded toward the dance floor, just like I used to do to her. When I faked like I was going to set my horn down and get up, she broke into a smile and waved her hand down by the side of her chair to tell me to sit down, and she mouthed, "No, No. No." We both had big smiles by then.

There was little doubt that the high point of the music that night was her rendition of "Willow Weep For Me," a song with a lot of pathos, a lot of feeling, and I don't think any of the great ones who have cut that tune, Billie or Ella or even June Christy, ever shared as much of the loneliness in it as Ginger did that night. When she stepped back to the mike to pick up the second chorus, almost everyone had stopped moving and were just holding each other and listening to her; you remember any of those lyrics?

"Gone my lover's dream,

Lovely summer dream

Gone and left me here

To weep my tears into the stream.

Sad as I can be.

Hear me willow

And weep for me.

Willow weep for me."

I don't think there was a woman there with dry eyes – and some of the men. She killed it that night.

We closed the last set with Miller's "Serenade in Blue" just like we used to do, and although it may seem a bit soupy, there were an awful lot of contented faces floating around the dance floor at the end of the evening. There was a terrific round of applause, and Martha and her new husband ran up on the bandstand and hugged Frank until the tears were running down both his cheeks, and then the applause got even louder. Then the bridegroom came around and shook all of our hands.

Afterward, everyone was just sort of milling around; you know that feeling when you've had a really great time, and now it's over, but you just kind of hang around because you really don't want it to end. I think the senior Babcocks may have had a once in a lifetime experience because I'm pretty sure that they expected this "my brother's band wants to play for our wedding" thing to be a small disaster that they would have to be gracious and tolerate, but it turned out not only to be a lot of fun but a rather moving experience. I'm judging this from the fact that they cornered Frank for about five minutes, and Mr. Babcock had his hand on Frank's shoulder most of that time, and before they split, Mrs. Babcock hugged Frank around the waist and then patted his chest about a dozen times as they were leaving.

Brothers Paul and Jimmy were helping us tear down, and most of us guys were sort of making promises to keep in touch better from now on while we were putting our horns away. Ginger was surrounded by one group after another, who felt like they absolutely had to talk to her about how great she had made their evening. But after a while, it really was all over, and it was just us, just Frank's band, that was left standing around in this big empty ballroom; just like old times … but so much *not* like old times.

About then, Libby and a couple other wives came in and asked if we were ready to go; I wasn't ready to go, but I didn't know exactly how to explain that, so I said, "Yeah, sure, why don't you get your coat, and I'll meet you out front," and the other guys said something like that and we all went to get our horns. Frank and Dolores and Ginger were all leaving early tomorrow, and I didn't want any of them to go; this was all too good to let go of so soon, so I was kind of lagging behind, and finally it was just the four of us. Frank and Dolores and I hugged and said all those nonsense things you say to friends you really love when you know you're not going to see each other for a long time, and then they left, and it was just me and Ginger.

I was afraid to speak; I was afraid to move. I was afraid to touch her for fear she would walk away, and I'd never see her again.

We just looked at each other, and then she stepped in close, took my hand in both of hers and looked into my eyes. She must have known she was the only woman I had ever loved … would ever love – because she said, "I know, Wally, I know … and I'm sorry … I think it probably should have been us all along."

She walked away, and I never saw her again.

The End

THE DANUBE

Ginny

We met about six or seven months ago when my girlfriend, Astrid, stood me up for a lunch date, so I ended up eating alone at a table next to this nice looking older guy, and he started talking to me, and he seemed nice, and he was pretty funny, and he suggested that we meet there for lunch the following week, and he promised "not to stand me up." Well, I did, and we started having lunch every once in a while, and then he asked me to go to the theatre, then he started taking me to films and occasionally to dinner, and we hugged and kissed, but he was always very polite and never got grabby or anything. He was a good bit older than me, probably in his fifties, and he didn't seem to have any kind of work schedule, and he was kind of vague about what he did for a living. He did say he worked for Cunningham & Walsh when he was in New York, and I found out they were an advertising firm, but when I later asked him if he was in advertising, he said, "More like Public Relations." When I asked him about DC, he would only say that he "worked on K Street with a bunch of people who were not as smart as they thought they were" – so that didn't tell me much either, and he came out here ten years ago to do *something* for Sony Pictures, and all he would say about that was, "it was rather boring."

I went to City College, and I went on a field trip to DC once, and my parents took my brother and me to Cabo San Lucas for a week, and I've been all over California, but I felt like I'd hardly traveled at all compared to him. He'd spent time in China, in Greece and Turkey, all over Europe, parts of Central America, and lived in New York City and DC. And now he wanted me to travel with him to Prague and cruise down the Danube for two weeks. I'd got enough extra days coming that I could get away for the two weeks and the way he talked about it, it sounded like a wonderful trip; it was just that he didn't talk about the sleeping arrangements, and I wasn't really comfortable with that. But he convinced me that I should get a passport just in case I ever did want to travel, and he helped me apply for one and even paid for it, so I didn't argue.

He knew that I worked in the lingerie department of Robinson-May and where I went to college, and that I lost my parents, and a lot about what I liked to do and what kind of friends I had, but I realized now that I didn't really know anything about him. Like, last week, after lunch he said, "Let's go talk to a travel agent about our trip," and when I told him that I hadn't really agreed yet, he said that was alright, this might help me make up my mind. The travel agent was this really pretty blonde woman, probably in her late thirties, who ran over to him as soon as we came in and gave him a big kiss right on the mouth. She seemed delighted that I was going with him and always asked me what I thought about the different side trips that she was working out. The more she talked about the trip, the more terrific it sounded, and she kept saying what a wonderful time I was going to have. She booked us a suite with separate bedrooms at the hotel in Prague, so that was a good sign, but it turned out that the only cabin available for the cruise was an Owners' Cabin, and he said "twin beds" and she said "of course" So, it looked like, *if* I was going, we'd be sharing a cabin but not a bed. I was still not sure how I felt about that. After everything was settled, she gave him a big hug and a peck on the cheek and said, "Call me, anytime." After we left, I asked him if he had taken her out, and when he said yes, I asked him where (thinking it was probably a real fancy restaurant), and he said … "Lisbon."

But that's what I mean – I just didn't know anything about the kind of life that this guy led, and he seemed so different from any of the guys I knew. What bothered me, I guess, was that I didn't want to have to "pay" for this trip by sleeping with him, and yet seeing Europe with a guy with this kind of experience was a chance I would never have again in my whole life. It's not as if he was gross or anything, and he's really not that old. I was having a tough time trying to work this out, and the time for the trip was less than two weeks away, and my passport had just arrived. His last name was Carnegie, by the way, David Carnegie.

———————

Well … here I am in Prague.

We flew first-class to Munich and then, after David checked a briefcase at the airport, we got on a little plane about an hour later, and arrived here at the hotel about 1:30 this afternoon. I've got to tell you:

first-class is the way to travel! I'd never had so many people asking me if there was *anything* they could do for me, and the seats turned into beds with little curtains around them and the stewardess woke me up with a cup of steaming hot chocolate, and a warm washcloth and a heated towel. The night before, we had cocktails and champagne with dinner (which was *squab*!) and two "nightcaps," so I had no trouble at all sleeping.

There was a big black Mercedes sedan and driver waiting for us at the airport, and we were staying at the Klarov (which they call a "boutique hotel"), right on the river in the heart of downtown. The Suite was on the top floor with this huge central room with a big long balcony where you could see castles and lots of the river and the countryside, with our bedrooms on opposite sides. As soon as we arrived, he had a couple of messages and said he had to meet these people, so he arranged for me to have a massage plus a mani-pedi, and when I got back to the suite there was this real tall, thin man with a goatee that he introduced as Count Strausberg. He was very polite, with bowing and hand-kissing and all that. David just said that he was an old friend who was slightly down on his luck. Then we walked to dinner, about a half a block away, came back and had a couple of drinks in the hotel garden and he kissed me goodnight and went to his room, saying he had some phone calls to make.

It was a sort of a whirlwind day, and it just seemed a little overwhelming, so that's why I decided to keep a kind of diary while I was there. I wasn't really worried, it's just that David seemed to have stuff to do that didn't concern me, and that was not at all what I

expected. Well – tomorrow would probably be entirely different. So …
Good Night, Diary.

The two other nights in Prague were much like the first night – after dinner back at our suite, David poured us both some brandy and then kissed me goodnight and went to his room to "make some calls." But the two days in Prague were marvelous! When they talk about the Prague Castle, it's not like a castle at all, it's like a small city with gardens and churches and little palaces, and there's another palace right in the town square, which looks like something out of a Disney movie. The food is great, I guess, but so rich I didn't see how they could eat like this every day. We took a cable car 1000 feet up to Petrin Hill where they had a little Eifel tower and a house of mirrors that's really fun; David was laughing out loud in there. The following day, before we took a limo down to Passau to board the Princess riverboat, he took me to a Beer Hall that is something like 500 years old and made me taste the beer that they are famous for; it was awful – bitter and thick – so I only had one taste and we left, but he wanted me to see the place.

So, there I was, nestled in my twin bed, writing in my "diary" while David was out on our private balcony sipping brandy and reading his Kindle. We had dinner on board and then listened to a piano player in the lounge and had a couple of drinks, and then when we came back to our cabin, David went into the bathroom and changed into pajamas and a robe, kissed me goodnight, and went out on the balcony. If I was worried about there being too much "romancing" on this trip, I was a little surprised to find out that there may be very little or none. So …
Good Night.

Passau is really quaint, and we walked all around the downtown area, and that night we went to an organ concert in the Cathedral, and when we came back to the boat there was a messenger who handed David a fat brown envelope, which he had to sign for. He said it was just the money that he had lent the Count in Prague. Then in Salzburg, the granddaughter of the von Trapp family from "The Sound of Music" gave a concert in the afternoon and then came aboard that night and conducted a sing-a-long. I couldn't believe how much fun that was; some of the songs were in German and some in French but a lot in English that I knew, and David could apparently speak both German and French, and everyone was laughing and buying drinks for everybody else, and they didn't shut us down until 2:30 in the morning.

The next day we were in Melk in the morning to see an ancient Benedictine Abbey. I couldn't believe how small the monks' rooms were; they were like a jail cell with just a low cot and a stool, and then to Durnstein in the afternoon for a wine tasting. After the wine tasting, David asked me if I had brought a bathing suit, and I hadn't, so he took me to a shop just off the square, gave me a credit card, and left me there because he said he had to meet someone, and I would be bored. Well, I found about four that I really liked it, and by the time I decided, he was back and took me to a tiny French café for dinner instead of going back to the boat. It was really tiny and crowded, there were only eight small tables, but he had made a reservation, and he and one of the waiters seemed to know each other. I say "seemed" because the whole evening was in French. When I asked him who he met, he said it was an old business associate who was kind of a bore. I asked him why the bathing suit, and he said we would have a nice long cruise to Vienna the next day, and he thought the sun deck would be a great place to spend our afternoon. When we got back to the boat, the bedtime routine was pretty much the same: he changed, he kissed me, then sat on the balcony until I was in bed. Ho – hum. I thought maybe tomorrow I'd be a little friendlier and see if it was as easy for him to go sit on the balcony tomorrow night. Well … Good Night, Diary.

The next morning, he went to breakfast before I woke up, and when I got to the dining room he was sitting with a nice-looking older woman, maybe about his age, and they were talking about a hotel in Tel Aviv. Her name was Allison Munroe and she was a retired travel agent, whose husband left her pretty well off, and she lived in Philadelphia, but mostly she just traveled around the world, sort of wherever she wanted to go. She was really curious as to why we were not going all the way down the Danube to the Black Sea. She didn't seem to believe me when I said I had to get back to work at a department store, but David said that he had to get back for a Board Meeting, and she had no trouble with that.

The afternoon on the sun deck was really nice and relaxing. David really liked my bikini and we sat and chatted; him in the shade and me in the sun and sipped ice tea. I asked him to rub my lotion on me, and he seemed to enjoy that; so maybe he was warming up a bit. The hillsides looked like carpets of green, with only one or two houses (or maybe they were castles?) every few miles. We went down for lunch and split a bottle of wine, and when we came back up, he rubbed lotion on me again, and after a while I fell asleep. When I woke up and went down, I finally found him in the lounge talking to the piano player. David told me that his "friend" was able to get us tickets to the Vienna Philharmonic Orchestra performance that evening at a hall called the Musikverein, so as soon as we docked, we had to grab a cab to the opera house. We would have dinner later.

The concert was a lot of Mozart and a short Bach piece, and it was really delightful. Although I have never much listened to classical music, everything I heard was really beautiful, and the theater was very classy with real soft seats, a neat bar in the balcony lobby, and ushers in white gloves. We went to a little restaurant in a German hotel for dinner afterwards, and David ordered me some kind of duck that was delicious and just melted in your mouth. But then a man came over to our table, and he and David spoke a couple of sentences in German and then David handed me a few Euros and told me to take a cab back to the boat because his friend was in trouble and needed his help. I didn't really want to leave him, but he said it was best because he didn't yet know how long it would take to straighten it out. He assured me that he'd meet me back in our cabin and I should just go to sleep, and he'd come as soon as he could. I gave him a big wet kiss to remind him what he was coming back for.

It was just before midnight when I got back to the boat, so I got ready for bed and put on a really cute pair of shorties and waited for him. He came back about one, and as soon as he came in, I went over and gave him a big soft kiss. He kissed me back pretty good, but then he pulled away, and told me he had to get something to help his friend, and he had a cab waiting, and he should be back soon. Then he went to the safe and got some stuff out, and then he came and held me and said he was sorry that he had not been paying more attention to me. He gave me a really sweet kiss and said he'd be back in an hour. Well, he wasn't back at two, and so at three I called the steward and asked him to tell the captain or whoever was in charge that Mr. Carnegie was missing. About a half-hour later the police came, and I told them the name of the restaurant and as much as I could about what happened. It was now almost four in the morning, and I hadn't heard anything, so I sat up in bed writing everything I could think of in my "diary," and I was waiting … and falling asleep … and I was scared.

———————

Michael

I've been lucky all my life, and I know it. I was shot once in Dublin when I was a Sergeant and shot again in Amsterdam after I joined Interpol; both times they laid me up for a while, but they missed any vital organs. I would have been called in on this one anyway because it was "Carnegie," but I got a lucky break because I was in Munich for a face to face with Jesse Gruber after the German branch picked him up trying to get on a plane to Argentina. His disguise was a good one, and I hadn't seen him in almost six years when I first suspected him of dealing in stolen paintings. He's a slick one, and of course he has no fingerprints, so Munich wanted me to do the ID. Since I was there, it was a short hop to Vienna. Interpol called me at six a.m., and I was on the scene before eight. Lucky.

On the flight, I started reviewing my file on Daniel Harvey, who I strongly believed to be the con artist who was currently calling himself "Carnegie." I had been following his trail for nearly twelve years and knew of his operations as far back as thirty years ago. When I first came into Interpol, my mentor Fergus McCann, assigned him to me and told me "he's as sneaky as a snipe." Whatever kind of animal he was, he had swindled over 16 million American dollars by our count, out of various unsuspecting victims in America and Europe and never been prosecuted. I got the ping when he left LA a few days ago, and then one when he arrived in Munich and then another when he arrived in Prague; again with a female traveling companion. Nothing more until this morning.

Daniel Harvey was born in Liege, Belgium, in 1955 of a German father and a French mother. Both were killed in a car crash when he was fourteen, and he went into foster homes for the next four years. Belgium Social Services was eventually the place that identified his fingerprints. How and exactly when he came to America is unknown, but "Harvey Daniels" was a page at the UN building in New York in 1978 and 1979. His first scam that we know of was in New York where he was operating as a stockbroker, under a different, name and managed to walk away with just over two million dollars from eight victims, none of whom "could believe it was that nice man." His name then was Gordon Wellington. In Washington, DC, he posed as a lobbyist for the Logging Industry and somehow managed to siphon off just over 500 thousand dollars a year for five years before he simply disappeared. That fellow was Grant Jefferson. In Hungary, Boris Shedecker represented himself as the real estate lawyer for the Strausberg family and sold over eight million Euros of property that he never owned.

That was when Interpol got involved. Similarly, in San Francisco, Buddy Mayer, Jr. sold classic cars he never owned to the tune of over four million. And my latest update had him now in the Los Angeles area but doing a lot of traveling abroad under the name of David Carnegie. He was in London and Paris for five days with a dark-skinned beauty carrying an Israeli passport about six years ago, and two years ago, in

Lisbon and Porto for six days with a pretty blonde American. I followed them in Porto for three days but saw nothing but tourist stuff. Now I had word that "David Carnegie" was in Vienna … and he was dead.

An old buddy whom I hadn't seen in years grabbed me in a bear hug the minute I stepped off the plane. Franz Kempen was about the size of a small bear and twice as hairy, and one of the great beer drinkers of six continents. I can't vouch for Antarctica. He and I worked a triple murder in Rhode Island when he was on loan to the U.S. branch and I was following the killer from Liverpool. We got him, but then we went out for a drink – that was my mistake. Franz drank everyone in the bar under the table and then started tossing those tables around until both of us got arrested. Neither of our home offices was very happy with us. My next mistake with Franz was this morning when he told me he had just been made Detective Inspector and I told him it was no big deal because I had held that rank at Interpol for the last three years. He hit me on my upper arm so hard it almost knocked me over.

"Asshole."

"Pussy."

I knew we were going to get along again just fine.

Franz was a member of the Austrian Gendarmerie when we met, but now all branches of Austrian crime investigation are simply under the Federal Police. He called Interpol as soon as he found ID on the body showing "David Carnegie" because Carnegie was on our current *"notice"* list. The corpse had no face left, and the ends of his fingers were burned off. On our drive to the docks, he filled me in on all the details he had since the body was found at 3:45 in the morning. Time of death was between one and three a.m., and the Coroner was certain that acid had been used to destroy the facial features and the fingers; what kind was yet to be determined: blunt force trauma with some sort of cudgel or club was the COD. I wanted to see the body, but Franz said that here the Coroner had sole custody of the body until he completed a full autopsy, and there was no way around him. Also, there was a full packet of pictures of the body and the scene back at his office that I could see any time, so he thought the best route was to the scene of the crime and then the restaurant where Carnegie was last seen and then to the riverboat where statements from everyone on board were being taken by two of his detectives. So far no one had been released, but there was a lot of huffing and puffing about passengers' vacations being ruined, and Franz' boss had already received a pressure call from the Burgermeister's office. The ship was scheduled to stay in Vienna until 7:00 p.m., and "everyone" would be much happier if the boat and its passengers were cleared by then.

The body was found in a narrow separation between two small wooden buildings no more than 50 meters from the pier where the riverboat was moored. I could see the boat from where we stood. The victim was apparently headed to the boat or from the boat; no witnesses, of course. So – was it someone who followed him from the restaurant or someone from the boat who knew he was out and waited for his return? It was certainly not a crime of convenience or chance, with all that mutilation. This was certainly someone who knew him, if indeed this was really Daniel Harvey. Franz pointed out what could well be drag marks just passed the opening, so the perpetrator may well have concealed himself in that passageway, but he left no indications to confirm that theory. I would have to wait and check the photos to see if the position of the body offered any more suggestions. We checked both the buildings and found nothing, but I asked Franz to have some of his men check all the buildings along this pier for signs of a break-in, but for now, the scene of the crime didn't tell us much.

The Grand Hotel Wein was pretty grand indeed, and Franz and I were about as welcome as a pair of lepers. One of the Assistant Managers herded us into a small room behind the Concierge's desk and, after offering tea or coffee, said he would bring in any staff members we wanted to see, so as not to interrupt guests who were still breakfasting in the dining room. Very thoughtful. Franz had contacted them earlier and told them to have last night's dining staff on call this morning. I don't know where they were, but when we asked to see the Maître d', the bartender and the waiter who served Mr. Carnegie, each of them popped in within two or three minutes. Talk about discreet; if any of them were any more non-committal there would have been absolute silence. They were all in agreement that "this lovely couple" had dinner and then the young lady left and the gentleman was joined by another gentleman and then they both left together. Who the other gentleman was is an unknown; none of them "ever saw him before?" Could you describe him? "Average height," "average looking," "medium brown hair." Did there seem to be any tension between the two men? "Not that I noticed," "Not noticeably," "I didn't notice any." Jesus, Mary, and Joseph! ... were all these guys deaf, dumb and blind? ... Nobody knows *anything?* The only thing we learned from this exercise in frustration was that both men left together, and his "lovely" dinner companion left earlier. W now had two people who were the last to see him alive, and we needed to find them both. I suggested that Franz go back to his office and start running down taxi companies that had made runs from the Wein to the docks, and any late runs from the docks. I'd head to the riverboat, and he could join me later.

These riverboats are really quite beautiful, and the River Princess may have been one of the classiest. A reception area that was as big as a hotel lobby and a huge lounge that was a little heavy on "green" for my taste, but certainly well-appointed. When I arrived, the lounge was packed with all those sightseers who were in varying degrees of irritation because they weren't out enjoying the sights of Vienna. I introduced myself to Detective Johann Dietrich, and he brought me up to date on the interview process which he and his partner, Kirk, had just concluded. All of the crew was confined to the ship since about 3:30 this morning, except for the Chef and two kitchen helpers whom the Captain vouched for so they could get to the local market for fresh supplies this morning. He said he anticipated that there may be extra feedings today. All three of them had already returned. Twenty-two crew members went ashore last night, and all of them had signed back onboard before one o'clock in the morning. Of the 116 passengers, only "Carnegie" and his companion had left the boat last night. All the others attended a Captain's Party in the dining room, followed by a wine and brandy tasting in the lounge which lasted until two a.m. There were very few passengers who had any contact at all with our victim. Johann suggested that while I talked to them, he would send his partner back to Headquarters, where staff personnel were available to start verifying the identity of all the passengers through their respective Embassies, and he would stay with me to give whatever local assistance I needed. He also told me that Kirk had checked "Carnegie's" room but couldn't find his toothbrush or comb and brush for DNA comparison (which was very odd), so he got socks and underwear and took them back to the lab. I reminded myself to tell Franz that Johann had a good head on his shoulders and was a first-rate detective. It was now twelve noon, and the speaker system announced that "luncheon was being served" in three languages. The lounge started to empty almost immediately, and a steward brought a tray for Johann and me and set us up at the bar. I realized that I had nothing but tea for the last six hours, but before I could dig in, the interviewees started to arrive.

The first passenger I talked to was an American named Allison Munroe, who had breakfast with Carnegie and his lady friend. She claimed they had never met before and could tell me very little about either of her breakfast companions. She was traveling down the Danube and was quite concerned about being delayed in Vienna. I found her nervousness rather difficult to read, and that always bothers me, but she seemed an unlikely stalker, so I thanked her and moved on. The piano player was an Austrian from Vienna who was friends with a French Horn player in the Vienna Symphony and was able to get tickets for Carnegie and friend to last night's concert. He also attended the concert, had drinks with the horn player after, but signed back onboard at 12:45 this morning, which Johann had verified. That's fifteen minutes before the earliest time the victim might have been killed. He also claimed not to have known him or the woman before the cruise started. We could check his whereabouts with the horn player, but he didn't seem a likely candidate for the murder either. I told Johann I really wanted to get something to eat before I saw the "lady friend" and I wanted to give Franz time to get here so he could sit in with me when I questioned her.

She seemed our best chance of getting some details about Carnegie's background and some information about where he had been and whom he might have seen on this trip. I took a few minutes to myself and scarfed down a great cup of bean soup, maybe lentil, and a quiche that was terrific – both re-heated by the ubiquitous barman, who was the one serving drinks here in the lounge until two. I needed to tell Franz that we now may have to check out the concert hall since that was the victim's next to last stop. This trail was getting wider rather than narrower; not a good thing.

When Franz arrived, he brought the photos of the crime scene with him. I told him about the concert hall, and he told me that the only taxi pick-up at the Grand Hotel Wein that dropped a fare at the docks was clocked at 11:50 last night, and it was a young lady. Carnegie's whereabouts just got murkier: was he with the man he met in the restaurant? Did they drive down here together? Did his friend drop him off and someone else kill him? We were not getting any closer to unraveling this story. We were going to take a close look at Carnegie's cabin before seeing the girl, but right then, our best hope was that this companion could lead us in the proper direction.

Wilhelm Haas

When I first saw him sitting in my dining room in Passau, I could hardly believe it, and I had no idea what to do. I wanted to grab him and strangle him, but I got hold of myself. First of all, I wasn't absolutely certain; he was clean shaven, no van Dyke beard, and he was older of course, and had put on a little weight, and his hair was brown with touches of grey, not the clear Aryan blond of before. I snuck a picture of him with my phone and sent it to my brother, Werner, in Baden. Werner texted me back immediately: "That's him – that's Shedecker." Werner sent his picture to two other couples in Austria who were ripped off like us, and both of them agreed it was him.

Then we started trying to figure out what we were going to do about it; what *could* we do about it? The police were no help last time when we realized that we couldn't own the property that we thought we bought because it all belonged to the Hungarian government. The best we could hope for was that we could get him arrested on a fraud charge, but that was 12 years ago; was there a statute of limitations on that? Besides, that was not enough, he had changed our lives drastically; some of us had borrowed large sums, which we were still paying off to get in on that deal. All of us became destitute overnight; one man hanged himself. I thought of poisoning him, but I had no idea how to do that without being discovered, and Werner said for me not to even think like that. He said he would drive up to Vienna when the boat arrived there and meet with Shedecker and see if he could open a discussion on some sort of settlement. The two other couples agreed that this would be a good place to start. I told them he was traveling under the name of David Carnegie and that I would keep them informed of when and where he was going as well as I could.

When Lantz, the pianist in the lounge, was eating dinner in the crew mess, he told me he was going to the concert to see a fellow musician and that he had got tickets for Carnegie and his lady. I called Werner, and he said he would watch for them when they left the Musikverein and find a time to talk to him. Around midnight he texted me to say that he was meeting Schedecker in a bar near the Hotel Wein and that he was going to drive him back to the boat after they had settled a few things. Then, the next morning, I heard that Carnegie had been found dead, and I'd got no word from Werner, and all my calls were going to voice mail. There were police all over the boat, questioning all of us. I played the part of the "dumb cook," of course, but I hadn't been able to find out anything else. I was going crazy!

Ginny

It couldn't have been any more than six o'clock when there was this pounding on my door, so I jumped out of bed, and there was the cabin boy saying how sorry they were and this policeman in a funny uniform telling me to get dressed and come with him. I tried to find out about David, but he said "the detective" would explain everything. As soon as we left the cabin, another policeman put tape all across the door, and the first one led me to the lounge where he handed me over to "the detective" named Johann Dietrich. He was very courteous, asked me to sit with him. He and told me that a body had been found that had been identified as David Carnegie. I was stunned. I didn't know what to say. I started crying, and he gave me a handkerchief and just let me cry for a while. Then he asked if I had any idea why Mr. Carnegie would be out walking on the pier at one or two in the morning. I told him all about last night and the German man. He thanked me, asked if there was anyone I wanted to call or if there was anything he could do for me, but I couldn't think of anyone or anything. He then led me to the Captain's quarters, told a steward to bring me some breakfast, and told me to wait there until his superior came by to talk with me.

Hours went by. It was like I was suddenly in a movie or something; nothing at all like this had ever happened to me; I didn't know what to think — even what to feel. I liked David, maybe a lot, but I realized more strongly than ever that I really didn't know anything about him, and now he was dead? It didn't seem real. And the next person who knocked on the Captain's door didn't help any. Detective Inspector Franz Kempen looked like something out of the Grimm's Fairy Tales; he'd got muddy-brown hair down to his shoulders and a beard so full that it looked like just his eyes were peeking out from some kind of an animal suit. He spoke very politely, but he has such a guttural accent that everything sounded a little bit like a threat. He introduced me to Detective Inspector Michael Murphy, who was kind of soft-spoken and attractive — in a beat-up sort of way — and he asked if I was comfortable because they had a lot of questions for me.

We three settled in with tea for the two men and coffee for me, and I started to tell them everywhere we had been and everything we did. They didn't seem interested in much of anything that happened before we arrived in Prague, but afterward there were three things: all I could remember about Count Strausberg; the messenger and the brown envelope in Passau, and especially the German-speaking gentleman from last night. I described each of them as best I could, and they both took notes but were very non-committal about whether what I told them was of any help. Detective Murphy also asked me my impression of Allison Munroe, and I said that I didn't like her. When he asked if I trusted her, I had to admit that I didn't. Then they started to ask questions about how long David and I knew each other and if we had traveled together before. Then Detective Kempen started asking if I had a lot of credit card debt or any financial obligations, but when he asked if I expected to be "a little bit better off" when this trip was over, I got mad, because that sounded like he thought David was paying me to go with him or something like that.

Then Detective Murphy said he was sure his friend had not meant anything offensive and asked if I could tell them anything more about why the safe was empty, except for my passport and my plane ticket? And did I know what happened to the brown envelope? Well I guessed that David took whatever was in the safe to his friend last night, but that didn't seem to satisfy them, because they both just sat there looking at me. I asked what was in the envelope, and they wouldn't tell me, or maybe they didn't know. Then he asked me if I knew of any other parcels that David had picked up or dropped off on our trip, and I couldn't think of any until I remembered he had checked a briefcase in Munich when we arrived there. They noted that. Then Murphy said: "Franz?" ... and the hairy one said "Nein" and they both thanked me, and the big one told me that it was likely I would have to stay in Vienna even if the ship and other passengers were allowed to leave this evening. When I asked what he thought I did and was I under arrest, Detective Kempen said I was "a person of interest" until a number of details were cleared up. He said I could return to my cabin as soon as the tech crew was finished, and he was very sorry for the inconvenience. But I didn't believe that. When they left, a sketch artist came in, and I described the German man to her, then the Count and then the messenger, and I thought she did a great job because all three looked a lot like I remembered. It was then nearly five o'clock, and I was sitting in my cabin wondering what was going to happen to me and how I got into all this mess … and how was it going to end … and now I was getting really scared.

Michael

After we left the girl, Franz and I went on the top deck to get some air and try to put some pieces of this puzzle together. We asked Johann to join us, and we hoped that in bringing him up to date it might help us clarify where we stood. We found a spot aft, away from the grumbling passengers, and ordered tea; Franz had a flask of schnapps, which helped bring the tea to life. We first told Johann about Count Strausberg; he already knew about the German speaker at the restaurant. They told me there hadn't been a "Count" Strausberg since the late eighteenth century, although the Strausbergs were an ancient and wealthy family in Hungary. So that "Count" character may have had some connection to Harvey when his alias was Shedecker, and he was selling bogus property. The "messenger" didn't offer much promise because he could easily have been legitimate. That made the German speaker at the restaurant our primary target for the moment, with Miss Virginia ("please call me Ginny") Downs as a possible accessory. When the sketch artist brought up her portraits, none of us recognized the German, so Franz sent Johann back to headquarters to have it copied and put out on the wires as "wanted and dangerous." I told Johann that I had enjoyed working with him and looked forward to our next meeting. He said much the same, and he left. Franz recognized the "Count" as a small-time forger and sometime actor who could probably be found with a few phone calls to Prague, but he was sure he was no killer. Franz had another call from his boss putting the heat on him to get this boat out of Vienna by seven that evening.

When the road ahead is unclear, I've learned that the best place to go is back to the beginning; the beginning of the case, and the beginnings of the suspects. In this case: the crime scene photos of the body: the crime scene about fifty meters away: and better still, back to any of Harvey's previous victims who may be in this vicinity, because they might be looking for revenge. I had a list of Shedecker's victims in my files, but only three pictures to go with the sixteen names. None resembled our German, but Franz found a cook named Wilhelm Haas listed among the crew, and I had a Werner Haas on my list. We would talk to Wilhelm and see if there might be some connection. It was now five o'clock.

Michael – Franz – Wilhelm

"Your name is Wilhelm Haas?

"Ja."

"Do you know a Werner Haas?"

"Mein brudder."

"English, please."

"Yes, he is my brudder."

"Have you been in contact with him lately?"

"No."

"Do you know where he is right now?"

"No."

"Do you know where he lives?"

"Ja – in Baden."

"That's very close – don't you visit when you come to Vienna?"

"Nein – I come through here every fortnight."

"And?"

"We see each other on holidays is mostly all."

"When was the last time you talked to him?"

"Oh … maybe two – three weeks."

"You have any idea where he might be right now?"

"Nein … no, none."

"So, we should be able to find him at his home in Baden?"

"I don't know … yes."

"And where do you live when you're ashore?"

"Linz, Austria … near to Passau."

"Did you know the gentleman who disappeared last night?"

"Nein … no."

"Do you remember seeing him?"

"No … I don't much go in the dining area."

"Have you ever heard the name Shedecker before?"

"Shedecker?"

"Yes."

"Maybe – I'm not sure."

"Boris Shedecker cheated your brother out of a lot of money, twelve or so years ago."

"Aaaaaaaah Ja … that's the name … yes – I remember that name."

"Do you remember what he looked like?"

"Noooooo ... I was just a kinder – a child ... I never saw him ... my brudder told me about him."

"He's a lot older than you, your brother?"

"Yes – ten years almost older."

"So, you wouldn't know this Shedecker person if you saw him?"

"Nein ... No ... no."

"Well – thank you for your time – and if you hear from your brother, it is very important that you let us know immediately."

"Ja."

"You understand? Immediately."

"Ja ... yes – I understand."

"Okay – we will probably want to talk to you again. Please do not leave the boat."

Michael

As soon as we got back top-side, Franz got a call from the Coroner who had identified the acid as "muriatic," an acid often used to clean boat hulls when they are out of the water. Then he asked me: "You think he was lying?"

"Yes."

"Me, too."

"So, our probable killer is Werner Haas, no?"

"Let me see those photos of the crime scene."

We spread them out on the table, and I started to examine the body more closely. I carry a magnifying glass in my briefcase, and the first thing I noticed was that the victim had on neither a belt nor braces.

Strange. The next thing I noticed was that the coat sleeves seemed to be bunched up on both arms as if they had been pulled up to make them seem the proper length. Maybe that jacket didn't fit that body – maybe that wasn't Daniel Harvey at all! "Maybe Werner Haas is the victim – which I now think is far more likely." Franz seemed puzzled, so I explained what had sent me off on this path.

Only someone trying to conceal his own identity would go to all the trouble of mutilating a corpse so that only DNA could make the identification. DNA confirmation would take at least six to eight hours, at best, and even 24 hours sometimes, so we could assume the killer needed time to put his escape plan into motion. Leaving Carnegie's wallet and stuff was just to keep us focused here for as long as possible. Why would Werner Haas, or any other killer for that matter, want to make it hard to identify their victim? Hard to identify themselves, yes, but their victim, no. I was pretty certain now that Haas was the German in the restaurant and was willing to bet that he was now in the morgue, and Daniel Harvey was on his way to disappearing once again.

I believed that there were only two scenarios that would serve Harvey's needs at this time: one, that he needed to retrieve a "new" identity from that briefcase that he checked at the Munich airport, or two, that he and Alison Monroe knew each other before this trip, and she was going to be able to provide him with whatever he needed to slip out of the country undetected. I suggested that Franz have his men shadow the woman on her way down the Danube while I headed for the Munich airport.

Just then, Franz got another call from his boss. "He's getting a lot of heat to get that boat out of here. What can I tell him?" I thought for a minute, but I felt pretty secure about my current theory, even though there were a couple of loose ends. "Tell him to release the boat, and we'll take the cook and girl into custody until we get a positive ID on the body." Franz told the boss what he wanted to hear.

If Franz held the boat, he was going to take a lot of guff from a flock of people, and if letting the boat go turned out to be a big mistake, then Franz could always tell them that Interpol said to do it. If I was wrong, then Harvey was dead, and that was a good thing, and I would hang around and see if I could help Franz solve a local murder. Yeah, I was slightly out on a limb, but some of this was beginning to make sense to me, and I could take the heat. Harvey was a brilliant con-artist, but I figured him for an amateur killer, and now he had to do a lot of improvising. I felt certain that he would make some little mistake or tip his hand in some way; this was all new territory for him. Werner Haas had pushed him out of his well-planned comfort zone. I just had to stay focused and concentrate. And, of course, maybe get lucky.

We put cuffs on Haas, but I just took the girl by the arm, and by the time we stepped off the boat, the crew was busily making preparations for their departure, and for the first time since I had arrived, I actually saw some passengers with smiles on their faces. Life goes on, doesn't it?

Ginny

The only thing either of the two detectives would tell me on the way to the police station was that as soon as I got there, I could call the American Embassy. Well, I was pretty mad, and I kept asking them what they thought I had done, but all they would say was that I was "a person of interest" and they couldn't let me leave Vienna for the time being. When I got there the one named Murphy got out of there in a big hurry, and the hairy one took me to a little room with no windows in it and left a uniformed woman with me who said she could get me something to eat and drink if I wanted. I was hungry, but I told her I wanted to call the American Embassy first, so she took me to an office and got an outside line and handed me the phone and wrote the Embassy number on a desk pad.

When I told the man who answered the phone where I was, I was transferred to two other people before they even asked my name. Then they wanted to know why I was in jail. I explained all I could, and then they asked for my passport number, but the hairy one had taken it. I asked the woman if she would get it for me, but she said she couldn't leave me and that I should tell them I'd call back and then we could both get it together. I tried to explain this to the guy on the phone and asked if he couldn't just come over, and in the meantime I would go and get the number. But he said he would send someone over as soon as I gave him my passport number. Well that made me mad, and I just hung up, and then that made me madder still because now I had to do exactly what that woman had just told me to do. This was not going well at all!

I settled down after a few minutes, and we went to find "Detective Inspector Kempen," as this woman kept correcting me. I called him the hairy one. When we got to his office and I told him about the call, he was all, "So sorry," and "Dat's a shame," and like that and had me sit at his desk. He fished out my passport and gave me the number. Then he got the Embassy number from the woman and called them himself and gave me the phone and told her to get me some hot tea and a roll. But he kept my passport, and he still had my airline ticket.

So I had to go through three people again, but when I gave this one the passport number he was all apologetic and said he would have someone over here within a half-hour – but before I could hang up, Detective Kempen asked me to give him the phone, and he rattled off a lot of stuff in German which ended with him saying "Ja sure, Ja sure," and laughing out loud. When I asked him what was so funny, he just said that they were old friends. Which I didn't believe at all; I just knew it was something about me – and probably something nasty. But he told me to make myself comfortable in his office, and as he left, the woman came back with tea and the best darn sweet-roll I think I have ever tasted, but maybe I was just hungry.

Well, it was way more than a half-hour before this very classy looking woman from the Embassy, named Alma Ford Sinclair, came into the office and was very, very sympathetic. She had already talked to Kempen, and he assured her that I was in no trouble, but, "You seem to be in the middle of an ongoing investigation," so there was not much she could do to get me out of the station right away. She asked if I had money and a credit card, and when I said yes to both, she suggested that she book me into a hotel that was just two blocks from the Embassy, and when I was released, I could take a cab there. Meanwhile she would contact the airline to make certain that I would be guaranteed a later flight if it became necessary, and she would contact the riverboat to instruct them to pack my clothes and have them messengered to the hotel she booked. I would never have thought of all that. Then she asked if I would like her to order in some food from a nice restaurant or if she could get me anything else to help me get through this evening. I didn't really want anything to eat, and I couldn't think of what else she could do for me. She did give me the impression that, maybe, this could all be over by tomorrow, but she would only assure me that "the Embassy will be at your service as long as you are in Vienna," and gave me her card with her office and cell phone numbers.

And now, it was almost seven-thirty, and here I sat, drinking my third cup of tea and eating my second sweet roll, and wondering when the hell I was going to get out of all this. I wanted to go home. I wanted to go home now! I'd seen enough of their damn Danube!

Michael

It was now eight o'clock, and I was getting just a little bit worried that my plan to catch Daniel Harvey at the Munich airport could be a total bust, and if it was, Franz was going to be laughing his big, shaggy head off because Harvey was headed in his direction and I was the one on a wild goose chase.

We got back to his station and turned Wilhelm Haas over for booking, just before six, and after another rib-crushing hug from Franz, Johann and I got in his police car and went "lights on" to the Vienna airport. I got the 6:25 flight out of Vienna, and I was on the ground in Munich by 7:30, but if, as I believed, Harvey took Werner Haas's car, it's only a four-and-a-half to five-hour drive from Vienna to Munich, and he could have left as early as two a.m. So, where was he?

While I was in the air, Franz called to tell me that his crew had indeed found a shed near the boat that had been broken into, and there were two bottles of muriatic acid on the floor. When I got that news, I contacted Hans Huberman of the Bavarian State Investigation Branch, whom I knew slightly from phone calls and emails, but had never met. Luckily for me, he was pulling night duty, which was generally boring as hell, and he was glad to have something to work on. I briefed him on the background and my plan to stake out the Baggage Claim, and he assigned me a plain-clothes officer to sit through until six a.m. if need be.

The officer's name was Schuler, and after he introduced himself, he settled in on a bench just outside the Baggage counter with three newspapers, each in a different language, and his briefcase. He might be an interesting guy to get to know – but not right now. We set our walkie-talkies to the same frequency; he covered the front, and I borrowed a clerk's jacket and sat in the back with a good view of the counter.

The good news was that the item that I based this whole plan on was still there in the Baggage Claim: that briefcase that Virginia Downs remembered him checking there before they flew to Prague. There were only three items left on the shelves that were checked in on the date they arrived there, and only one of them was a briefcase. I believed that this was where his new identity lay, and I didn't think he was going very far without getting rid of his Carnegie persona and donning a new guise because any airport that could get him out of the Euro Zone would give Interpol a ping as soon as that passport was logged in. There may have been something else in the briefcase, but I couldn't see him taking the chance of carrying two identities with him down the Danube, nor could I see him traveling without a solid back-up plan in reserve in case something went wrong on this current caper. Of course, it was all just speculation on my part, but here is what I think happened.

Werner Haas confronted Shedecker in the restaurant, and somehow Harvey convinced him that it wasn't necessary to call the police because he could give him all of his money back, or something like that if they would go back to the boat and let him get the cash. Haas drove them to the docks, and Harvey went to the safe and pulled out whatever it was he was carrying in that "brown envelope" and everything else of his. He was also smart enough to take his toothbrush, comb, and hair brush because he knew it could slow down the DNA confirmation if we only had Touch DNA to work with and not anything directly from him. Then, while Haas was checking the money or was somehow distracted, Harvey bashed him in the head, dragged him into that passageway, changed clothes, broke into that shed and grabbed a bottle of the muriatic acid and went to work on Haas. Then he took the car keys and headed to the Munich airport to pick up his new identity. What else he had to do, or what might have delayed him, and for how long? I didn't know. That was what worried me – was he hooking up with Alison Munroe somewhere down the Danube? Then it was in Franz's hands. Or was he eventually coming here? Or … and this was what I hadn't really thought about: was he going to lay low somewhere in those middle-European countries? Even if I was right that he needed a new identity, he probably had a large amount of money with him; maybe he could buy a totally new set of ID's in the shadowy world of Austria-Hungary?

Well – I guess I am one lucky son-of-a-gun, and I'll tell you why that's true. First of all, at five minutes after ten, Daniel Harvey walked up to the Baggage Claim counter in the Munich airport with a military crew-cut and bleached blond hair, dressed in a work shirt and jeans, to claim item "T16019." So, this new look was what caused the delay. He certainly looked different from the "Carnegie" character, but fairly easy to identify for anyone who knew him. The clerk got the briefcase, and as soon as Harvey picked it off the counter and turned around, I called Schuler, and he grabbed him and cuffed him. It was that quick!

Harvey was yelling that he was "just a messenger," and "What is this all about," but when I came out and said, "Daniel Harvey, this officer is arresting you for the murder of Wilhelm Haas," he got very quiet. Schuler popped open the briefcase for me, and there was a full set of IDs and credit cards in the name of Brandon Collingsworth, citizen of Canada, with a picture of a guy with blond hair and a crew-cut. Also, about twenty thousand Euros, and these were real; I say that because when we fished a set of car keys out of Harvey's pocket, they led us to a car in the parking lot that had another briefcase in the trunk that contained one brown envelope and one white envelope, each with almost one hundred thousand counterfeit Euros in hundred denominations. We had him cold on possession of counterfeit currency, and his evening wasn't over yet. I had to smile because the second thing was that, ten minutes ago, Franz had called to tell me that the Coroner had confirmed that the clothes on the body were from the same person as the underwear and socks retrieved from Carnegie's cabin and that Wilhelm Haas was the murder victim. So there – we had Harvey at the scene of the crime.

Schuler called to have someone pick up the car, and we went back to the Bavarian Station to lock Harvey up, and I had a chance to meet Hans Hubermann, in person, who turned out to be a really neat guy. He looks a lot like Pierce Brosnan, has four kids, and a wife who is a Swedish knockout, judging from the photo on his desk. He played on the

German national soccer team for two years and just got his first Master's points in tournament bridge. I got all that background from Schuler on the drive back. Somebody should do a movie about this guy! Also, he pulled out a bottle of Jameson from his bottom drawer to celebrate our collar. No wonder I like him. With refreshment in hand, I called Franz and told him we nailed it, and he could let both our "suspects" go. Then I called the home office in Lyon and reported the arrest of Daniel Harvey at 10:22 p.m. this evening by the Bavarian Police, but they asked me to hold because I was posted to another assignment. After they ran down the duty officer, he told me that I had been requested by the Los Angeles Vice Squad in the matter of a South American drug king-pin named Dellasandro DeGama, whom I had looked in the eye just twelve months ago at the Ramón Villeda Morales International Airport, in Honduras. Los Angeles said they hoped I could be there within the next two days, which suited me just fine; I'd never been to LA.

So, here was my plan. Get a hotel room and a few hours' sleep. Call Franz in the morning and find out when Miss Virginia Downs was flying out of Munich to LA and what flight she was on; I was pretty sure she would be anxious to get out of this part of the world. If my Interpol ID wouldn't get me a seat next to her, I'd bet my life that Hans Hubermann could get almost anyone in Munich to do pretty much whatever he asked. On a twelve-or–so-hour flight, who knew what could happen; "Ginny" and I might even become friends.

Hey – I'm a lucky guy, right?

THE END

PARIS

Paree!

The first time I was in Paris was when I was sixteen, and Father sent Mama and me there as my birthday present. Father sent us, but I'm sure it was Mama's idea because he never wanted me to stray outside the courtyard. Now, almost twenty years later, I'm going back – and again it's a present. Only this time it's a wedding present from my husband – or, at least he will be my husband tomorrow.

My first trip to Paris was like a dream, but weeks later, my life had changed drastically. That's why I've been apprehensive over the last few weeks; I felt like something terrible was going to happen; a catastrophe. Of course, I'm very happy to be getting married to a wonderful man like Jordon and, of course, spending five days in Paris with him sounds heavenly, but that other trip to Paris was a preamble to a radical change in all our lives, and there is something about that city that still seems foreboding.

It was just a bit over two weeks after Mama and I returned home, that we were forced out of the palace and found ourselves in Switzerland … and in exile. Father was no longer a King, nor Mama a Queen, nor my brother a Prince, nor me a Princess. And it all seemed to happen over-night. We left the palace at three in the morning and arrived in Lucerne just after sunrise. A few suitcases, mostly clothes, certainly no royal jewelry and no servants, and we're put up in this tiny Pensione. At least it seemed tiny to me. The first few months were a big shock for me, even though Father and Mama seemed to settle into these few rooms and carry on as if nothing much had changed but the geography. My brother, Marcus, and I had a lot to learn about taking care of ourselves and especially about the difference between *telling* people what to do and *asking* them. But our parents had always been very clear about our obligations to our subjects so – after a lot of blunders and more than a few scoldings, we began to figure out how to get along in this new society that we were dropped into.

Father had enough money in a Swiss bank to care for us for a time but, clearly, we were soon to become part of the "working class." We lived in Lucerne and learned to adapt to our new world for nearly a year before we finally came here to *this* New World and southern California. Lucerne is a beautiful city, right on the Lake and surrounded by the Alps. It seemed like there was a festival of some kind almost every month; lots of parades with tons of people in masks and costumes everywhere. It's a very easy city to walk around in, and almost everyone is very courteous and helpful. It was probably very fortunate for Marcus and me that we lived in Switzerland for so long because the Swiss are so polite compared to Americans, and we had time to adjust our perceptions of the world, without offending *too many* people.

So, maybe it wasn't a catastrophe, but it certainly was an abrupt change, and I don't want something like that to happen when Jordan and

I come back from Paris and start our new life together. Actually, the life our family has made here is more than pleasant, and life in the palace seems more and more like just a dream because all of us have found work that we enjoy and made many friends that we cherish. Father is a consultant for a foreign currency Exchanges and Mama seems to be involved in about a dozen charity programs. Marcus, it turns out, was apparently not wasting his time on all those video games because he's some kind of computer programmer now and is doing quite nicely. I don't want to see any of our lives change radically again.

While I was finishing high school, I started working after school in Francois' restaurant. Francois DeVere is a family friend, who is a chef, and was instrumental in getting us out of Europe and all the way to California. Francois took great care to start me at the bottom, and he moved me up very slowly, which I wasn't too crazy about at first. But I enjoyed working there so much that I made food service the center of my studies in college and, after following him to a couple of different venues, I set out on my own and now manage a very nice restaurant in Los Angeles. That is how I met Jordan, which would certainly never have happened if I had grown up as a Princess in my own country. So, maybe, everything does work out for the best, like my friend, Eamon, says.

Jordon's family owned land in Napa Valley, just outside Yountville, and they got involved in wine production many years ago. He tells me it's a great area for cabernet sauvignon. When his father died, Jordon took over and is running a boutique vineyard now that is developing quite a nice reputation. When we first met, he was thinking of putting in a small restaurant, and we talked about that a lot, and after we started making plans for me to manage it, we decided to get married. We think it will be the perfect size for us with just eight small tables plus a private room with a large, oval table. That's something I really wanted, because when we had formal dinners in the palace, we had this huge oval table where everyone could talk to everyone else, and I always had the best time getting to know whoever was visiting us. It's a special table like that which we hope will draw large parties, and my attention to service that we think will make our little restaurant a very unique place. Like Eamon says, "It's all in the details."

Jordan is a terrific guy, and I loved going up to Napa long before I met him, so when I went to a wine-tasting at his vineyard, his invitation to "come up anytime" was an easy one to respond to. Pretty soon I was making a trip up there almost every month, and he found some reason to come to LA about every other month. We had another connection because Jordan had studied winemaking in the Rhone valley for three months, and his French was quite passable, and French was my second language. I didn't think much about a long-distance romance, but after he asked me to come up and spend a week with him, we just started talking about how nicely our interests dove-tailed, and when he asked me to marry him – in French – it just sounded like we were a perfect fit, even though we had only known each other just over a year. When I told Eamon, he said, if I was happy, he was happy.

Eamon is … my dearest friend, although we could hardly be more different in every way. We met at a restaurant where I was working, and we started having lunch together, almost every week, and we've continued for over six years now. He is a bit older than I am, quite a bit. His world revolves around books and plays and writing, and I'm much more interested in being with friends and traveling and food and doing things that are fun. I grew up in a palace, and he grew up on a farm in Tennessee. I hate being in front of groups, and he spent most of his life as a trial lawyer. He likes white wines while I like reds; I like Country music while he likes Jazz and opera – and on and on. But we seemed to enjoy each other a lot and, maybe because he is so different, I found him … interesting. We email all the time, and we send a "good morning" or a "goodnight" note most every day. I already sent mine this morning …

When I told him about my early life, he said that it was clear that he had been sent to be the Princess' court jester – my "fool," – and it was his job to entertain me – and he really does. He makes up stories to tell me; he writes funny limericks and even wrote lyrics for a song about me. Also, he has a very generous sense of humor; he gets the biggest kick out of it when I tease him or catch him in a tiny mistake – he just roars – he thinks it's the best thing. There are times when he calls me his "recovering Princess," when he thinks I've been too demanding or critical of someone. He says, "Most people try to do their best – it may not be their fault if sometimes that's not very good."

He also asked me to question my parents about our ancestors. I can't remember any of my grandparents because they died when I was barely a baby, and I was never very interested in all that family history. He seemed surprised – and was quite serious when he suggested that I should find out as much as I could about the people who came before me. When I asked him about his childhood, he said that his parents deprived him of the opportunity of ever becoming a great artist because his childhood was completely happy and without trauma. He did share

their two pieces of advice that he always tried to follow: from his father –
"Be kind to *everyone*" – and from his mother, "Do it *now*."

I thought he was one of the gentlest people I have ever met, and he was always reminding me that he was old enough to be "my uncle Eamon." I guess he said that so that I wouldn't feel uncomfortable about the difference in our ages – or something like that – and I guess I don't because he's pretty affectionate, and I'm pretty relaxed about that. The only time I ever felt even the least bit uncomfortable was one night at my place when I fell asleep and woke up in his arms.

I know that sounds strange, so I have to go back a bit. Eamon cared for his invalid older sister when we met, and it wasn't until after she died, almost two years ago, that we ever saw each other any time other than at lunch. Since then, we have dinner once in a while, and he takes me to the theater, and occasionally to the Hollywood Bowl for concerts. One time, he brought a huge basket with two bottles of my favorite red wine, bagels and lox, a thermos of coffee and a pint of Bailey's Irish Cream (another of my favorites), and we nibbled and sipped all through the concert. I got a little fuzzy that night, but I'm pretty sure it was "Hollywood Movie Themes."

Also, he would get DVDs of old films that he wanted me to see, and we would come over to my place, watch the movie and then go out to dinner, or sometimes – like this time – we'd have dinner and then watch the movie. So – we were watching something that I couldn't get interested in – I think it was Jane Austin – and it was late – and I put my head on his shoulder and then I must have fallen asleep. When I woke up, I was lying across his lap, and he was holding me in his arms; he was smiling down at me, and I didn't know where I was or what was going on. It was very still … and we just looked at each other for what seemed like minutes – and neither of us said anything. Then he bent down and kissed me on the forehead and said, "Good night, love … see you tomorrow," – and he left.

I'm sure that Eamon loves me, but he would just never say it, and I'm sure that was because he felt he was too old for me. We never made love or anything like it, and all our kisses were brief, public pecks on the mouth. Well – all but one, months and months before I met Jason, and it told me all I needed to know: Eamon's love for me would always be there whenever I needed it.

So – like I said, Eamon is … different. Very different from Jordan. What I love is that Jordan and I can talk about food and wine for hours. We both have very busy lives. I work five full days a week and sometimes six, and he has a business that keeps him involved almost every day of the year. If it wasn't for Mama, we would never have been able to plan our wedding this well or this quickly. We're being married here, and Jordan has shipped down all the wine and champagne for the reception tomorrow night.

I've quit my job now, and as soon as we return, we'll both be busy getting our restaurant equipped and staffed and ready to open. That will keep both of us occupied for some time to come, and running it will put me on a much fuller schedule than I had before. But I'm sure Eamon and I … I was sure …

I have to stop writing now …

I just heard Jordan and Mama come in – they get along great – and they were out shopping together, so I'm guessing it was something for the wedding. I'll have to go downstairs and try to behave like a bride on the day before her wedding. They don't know about Eamon.

I will also have to stop lying to myself ... stop saying "is" instead of "was."

So, tomorrow I'll be married, and the day after I'll be in Paris ... and now I don't have to worry about any terrible changes in my life when I come back ... the worst thing possible has already happened. Earlier this morning, I got a phone call from Colin, Eamon's oldest son. Eamon died in his sleep last night.

THE END

NOT PHILADELPHIA

When I walked into that room what come to my mind was this play that we seen Betty's niece, Sharon, in over in Freyburg. In the play there's this fella has two families in two different towns and he comes home one night and there's one of his boys from the other town setting in his living room, and he takes this big looooong look at the kid and then he says, "Boy, you belong in Philadelphia." When I heard that, I laughed so hard they was tears coming out of my eyes. This time, seeing Dolly there in *my* living room, I sure didn't feel like laughing, but that was the first thing come across my mind: "You don't belong here."

I'll tell you how this got started.

Me and Betty been married about twenty years, and we was doing pretty well. We married right out of high school. When we started out, Betty was working at Roseanne's Beauty Parlor over on Maple, and now she was running the place, and Roseanne don't do much anymore but sit at the cash register. I was clerking in Uncle Charlie's Hardware Store up here on Main, and now I own that store, and I got a cabinet-making shop next door that does all them kitchen cabinets and bathroom vanity things for pretty much every builder in town. Running both shops takes up most of my day. We got a sixteen-year-old daughter, Crystal, who sorta' tolerates us if we don't ask too many questions. We'd moved into the old Crowder house set back up there on the hill off Cumberland, the year after old lady Crowder passed. We'd modernized the kitchen and both bathrooms, and the old place was looking pretty nice. We both took two weeks off in summer, and we'd just go on over to the lake and get us a cabin and do nothing much but fish and eat for the whole week. So, everything was, you know, pretty good; we had no complaints ... at least I didn't.

That summer, we threw a big party for Crystal's sixteenth birthday up at the house, and we had a passel of guests: a bunch of her friends and their parents, everybody from Roseanne's, all my clerks and a flock of folks from church. It must have been better than sixty of them. One of the ladies from church told me they was all out of plates for the barbeque, and so I was rootin' around in the kitchen and the pantry and I couldn't find anything that seemed to satisfy her, so I thought I'd go downstairs to the rec room and see if there was something down there that would make her happy. When I got to the bottom of the steps, there was Betty and Clyde Barnstable, sitting on the sofa, big as life. He jumps up like a scared rabbit, and they both are telling me "not to get upset" ... "don't do nothing crazy" ... and all like that. I'm standing there, and my mind is like a complete blank ... I can't imagine what the hell Betty is doing with this big dumb-looking idiot. I don't remember being angry, all I remember is being stupefied. Dumbo says he's "real sorry this had to happen" and he skedaddles up the stairs.

Betty starts telling me that, it don't really mean anything, – it's just that I don't never talk to her 'cause I'm always working at something or another. She tells me that she has needs that she wants to express and feelings that she wants to share, and Clyde is so understanding. When she went to the Pastor and told him that she was unhappy and felt so unfulfilled, he told her that she should spend some time talking with Deacon Clyde. "Unhappy"… "unfulfilled"… when the hell did all this happen?… and when did Barnstable become so helpful … as far back as I can remember he was always about as useful as a dry well.

Over the next couple of days, I find out that Betty has been unhappy for the last couple of years. She is tired of the life we been leading and pretty much bored with me and with working and with fishing and not having anybody around who "understands" her. So, I ask her, does she want me to leave, or what, and she says, "Well, maybe for a little while," so she can have some space. What she needs is to get out and meet more interesting people and not be tied down all the time. Well, I don't understand half of it, but … I figure if I let her do whatever it is that she thinks she wants to do, then maybe in a while Betty will come to her senses and forget about all this foolishness.

It don't start out too good because Betty joins this Women's Book Club and some Social Calendar thing at the Church and starts taking overnight field trips to Knoxville and Chattanooga and Nashville and Murfreesboro. The upshot is that she's not at home much at all. I've moved into Clem Wentworth's three-room apartment over his garage, which is walking distance from the Store. I decided to hire the Widow Tyler to come look after Crystal and the house because I never knew whether Betty was going to be home or out gallivanting. I don't know if she's still seeing that idiot, Barnstable, or not, but she does spend a lot of time around the Church. I'm busy running two stores, so I figure I can ride this out. Anyways, now I go bowling twice a week instead of once, and I stay at the store longer. I eat at home whenever Betty is out so I can spend some time with Crystal, but mostly I eat out. This has been going on for near a year now. Crystal's about to have her seventeenth birthday, and I'm still wondering whether this is going to be how my life is from now on.

One day, I'm having lunch with Crawford, my head carpenter, at the Square Forty Diner down on Route 127, when this new waitress come over to take our order. Crawford's eyes are popping out of his head, and he can't remember what it was he was going to order … (it's been ham and Swiss on rye for the last five years, that I can remember) … and he's mostly making a fool of hisself. I'm having a hard time not laughing out loud. We finally manage to order, but when she goes off, Crawford is all, "Boy Howdy – ain't that some looker?" and, I swear, he is perspiring like a pig. It's like he never saw such a pretty thing in his whole life before. Well, she is a nice-looking young woman, and when she come back with our food, Crawford is still trying to talk to her but now he's half tongue-tied and is not making a lot of sense. She sorta of smiles at me and rolls her eyes like this is getting embarrassing. Her name-tag says "Dolly," and I can see where that might be a fair description, but I'm hungry, so I shoo her away and think seriously about pouring a glass of water on Crawford. We manage to finish lunch without any more of his shenanigans, but when I'm paying the bill up at the cashier, she waves at us and says, "Bye, Crawford … Bye Mr. Thomas … y'all come back," … and I damn near have to push Crawford out the door, 'cause he now seems to be nailed to the floor.

Nothing would have it but Crawford is now driving down to the Square Forty every day to have his lunch, and all of us are hearing how he is working up to asking Dolly out to the movies. Crawford has not had a lot of luck with women, and that's a sad thing because he is honest as the day is long, has a good heart, and could provide well for a family, but he was not blessed in the looks department. To be charitable, on a good day he looks like a scarecrow with a bad haircut. But we were all pulling for him, until a kinda' odd series of events put the kibosh on his romantic interest.

Week or so after his first encounter with Miss Dolly, she come walking into the Hardware store looking for some household tools. Cyrus calls me up front to help her, and he hightails it next door to the Cabinet Shop to let Crawford know she is in the store.

Miss Dolly was explaining to me that her apartment needed some minor repairs, and she wanted some decent tools, when we heard this "crash" on the other side of the store. Crawford had stepped on a rake, which popped up and hit him square in the nose and knocked him back into a rack of spades and shovels. He was laying there, kinda' semi-conscious, with his bloody nose dripping all down the front of him — trying to smile up at Miss Dolly. 1 think that was what discouraged him from any further pursuit. Turned out that when I took him over to Doc Simpson's to have him patched up, the Doc said he might have a concussion, so I took him to the hospital, and they decided to keep him overnight. Miss Dolly went with him all the way to the hospital because I think she felt like she was the cause of it all. I thought that was pretty considerate of her, and since it was rolling up on noon, I asked her if I could buy her some lunch. She allowed as how that would be nice as long as it wasn't down at the Square Forty, so we went over to Parson's Hotel dining room.

I didn't think much more about Miss Dolly until about two weeks later she called and asked if I could give her some advice about real estate. That sounded like something I could do, so I thought I'd treat us both and invite her to dinner at The Old House, that little restaurant up to the north end of Washington Avenue. It's quiet, and they serve the best candied yams and turkey breast in a hundred miles. The next Sunday night, I picked her up, and we settled down to a fine meal. I asked her to order some wine 'cause it was pretty clear she knew a lot more about that stuff than I did, and whatever it was, I thought it was darn good.

The upshot of all this was that she had some money from the divorce settlement, and one of her customers, Bradley Snyder, was building some condos down below the highway off Alvin York and she wanted to know if I would take a look at them and tell her what I thought. I knew Brad, and we had put the cabinets in the two units he had finished. I said sure, and she said she'd like to go with me and that she had Wednesdays and Sundays off. We settled on Wednesday. She seemed pretty excited about this and real happy that I was going to help her out; when I dropped her off that night, she kinda surprised me by kissing me on the cheek.

There was an awful lot of people that I didn't know at Crystal's Seventeenth party; of course, all my folks and Crystal's friends and parents, but these other folks must have been Betty's new friends, and they all kinda looked at me like I had a bad case of warts. I don't know who the hell they thought was paying for all the food they were chomping down and all the booze they were guzzling, but Betty had ordered aplenty. She made sure she put her name on the card that I stuck on the windshield of the little VW that I got for Crystal. I didn't see no sign of Barnstable, which was a good thing, but Rev. Houghton and Betty seemed to spend a lot of time together, and he seemed like he was awful pleased to see me, considering I hadn't been in his Church for nearly a decade. I guess it was a pretty good party for most everybody there, but in a town our size most everybody knew Betty and I was living apart. That kind of hung around like a dead cat. Toward the end of the evening, I wanted to ask Betty if she was thinking that maybe we ought to get back together, but her and the Reverend and some others decided to go down to Angelo's for dinner. I never got a chance to talk to Betty at all. I reckon I was a little p-o'd, so I called Dolly and asked her if she would like to have dinner with me. We went to the Parson's Dining Room again, and I guess she could see that I was kinda glum or something because after dinner she asked me if I wanted to come home with her … and I did.

Meanwhile, Betty was avoiding me at every turn and spending more and more time with one of her clubs or societies. I began to feel like our marriage was slipping down the drain. Dolly had bought that condo, and Snyder had built seven more of them setting side-by-side. It was a nice place, and I spent some time with her there, but I still felt like I was a married man. I'm no "holier than thou," but I did feel like it wasn't right for me to be starting up with another woman, so that one night was the only time we were together … like that.

Soon I got a call from Betty saying she thought we ought to sit down and have a talk. We settled on a Wednesday night at our house around five o'clock. I told Crystal what was going on and asked her if she wanted to be there; she wasn't sure.

There were quite a few cars in the driveway when I pulled up, but I didn't remember that until I walked into the living room: here was Betty, yeah, and Crystal, okay, and Rev. Houghton, really … and … Dolly? – whoa! And that's when I thought about that "You belong in Philadelphia" thing. Like I said I didn't exactly feel like laughing, but it seemed to me that anything I said then was likely to make things worse, so I kept my mouth shut.

Betty said, "Why don't you fix yourself a drink and come sit with us and we'll talk." The drink seemed like a good idea. When I come back from the kitchen, I noticed that the Reverend was sitting in the chair that had always been my chair, so I swallowed that, and went and sat in that uncomfortable recliner thing that Betty bought me. I took a healthy swig of my bourbon and ginger ale … and I waited.

First thing Betty done was introduce me to Dolly McCallister who was a new friend of hers who had been a big help in getting her to face up to where she was in her life. I just nodded. She come to confide in Dolly about our marriage and how she was so unsatisfied with it. Dolly and the Reverend had helped her to see that she had to admit that her marriage was over and that she had to move on. She should start her life anew with a man who understood her … turns out, that man is Reverend Houghton… I took a long drink.

Everybody seemed to be looking at me, and Betty had stopped talking, so I figured it was my turn. I figured I better hightail it out of there before I said or did anything stupid, so I finished my drink, set it down real careful, and stood up. I said, "Well, thank you, Betty … I believe I ought to get going now, so – Good Night, everybody," and I went on out and got in my car and drove away.

Dolly called me Thursday morning, and asked me to come over because she wanted to talk to me. Well, I did and she did. I never had nobody in my life talk about "falling in love," or stuff like that, but that's what Dolly did. She said she never felt more comfortable or safer than she did with me. You won't hear no more on that subject from me.

Dolly and me got married, with Crystal as her Bridesmaid, the week that Betty and the Reverend went on their honeymoon. I don't have no idea how all us different folks happened to end up the way we have, but I'm pretty darn sure that all of us are in better shape than the fella with that other family in Philadelphia.

THE END

AN ANCIENT TALE

I can't be certain that what I'm about to share with you actually happened, or not, because I have found different versions of the story in three different places, and each has some slight variations. Also, the events related are of a somewhat mythical nature. However, since people from three different time periods have found it to be worth telling, I believe that there is some reason for this story to exist and to be passed on to any who have an interest in the strange or inexplicable.

The first time that I came across the story was in the Fordham Library on the Bronx campus in New York City while I was researching medieval documents in pursuit of a doctoral degree in European history. It was the summer of 2001, and I was on leave from Spring Hill College, a small Jesuit school in Mobile, Alabama where I had been teaching history for the last four years. The document that I came across was actually the latest version of this person's exploits, but I only learned that later. At first, this was merely a strange story told to a capuchin monk and transcribed by him, in Latin, on a scroll dated circa 1360 A.D. It was intriguing, but not germane to my studies, so I simply made a copy to take with me and thought about it only casually until two years later when what seemed to be a much earlier version of the story was brought to my attention by a former classmate, teaching at Georgetown, in Washington, D.C.

Charlie Boyle and I were college roommates when I was a junior and he was a senior, and we have kept in sporadic touch over the years; I had sent him a copy of the fragment I had found, as a curiosity. He is currently in the English department, and one of his students came across an unusual document at a Smithsonian Exhibit on Sumeria and did an essay about it as an assignment. The document was translated from the Latin Vulgate but had its origin in a Sumerian scroll, and it named the principal character in the piece I had sent to Charlie. This fragment was not in any discernible verse form, as was the later portion, I had found. It was dated circa 420A.D. Charlie sent me a copy, and I now had what seemed to be an earlier version of the story.

> *On the first day of summer sun, which starts to melt the winter snow, he came down from the mountain. He came down from the mountain, his shoulders covered with snow. He was tall as a small elder. He was tall as a bear. He was taller than his fellow-man, if still a man he be, by head and shoulder. His visage stern, but not unkind, and ringed with hair and beard of lightest brown. His armless tunic sewn from the skin of a mountain lion, for surely the cowl that hung down his back was naught but the mane of a lion. He was girded with the woven skin of a snake, and in that belt was a sharpened knife that seemed chiseled only from stone. It glistened like a snow-capped hill. In his left hand a cudgel of the darkest wood and in his right a clump of purple wildflowers held he there. And close by his heel, wherever he turned, was a wolf of green eyes, and fierce aspect, too.*

He had grown on the mountain, wild and untamed, yet all in his manner was only serene. Seldom seen but by a chance glance since that awful day when his parents were flayed. His parents were flayed to their death. Flayed when he was but a babe. Flayed by the Khan because they refused to send his sister, their daughter, to court. Flayed before the babe, and the sister taken. Seldom sighted in all those years between. And now he came to stand at dawn in the center of the square.

How he lived, none could know. They say he ate the air and drank the snow. He lived in the wild. He lived in the grass. He lived in the trees. He lived in the icy stream and in the rocky fields. Nor cave nor hut nor shelter large or small was ever found. How he lived and grew and flourished is simply the first of his mysteries. For here he stood in the center of the square as solid as the granite of the mountain, with the wolf-thing at his side, and spoke aloud. Now was gathered half the farmers from out the countryside, for word of this man-beast had traveled like the sparrow. And now he spoke for all to hear: "Tell the Khan to bring my sister to me."

All were hushed to see what next would transpire, for the Khan's men were seen among the crowd and some left to carry the message to the Khan. In short time came the Khan with many more and many weapons drawn open. The sister in the rear, chained and girded about among a host of guards. The Khan sent his soldiers forward to tame this brash intruder. As they came near, he raised the cudgel with his left hand and the flowers with his right; they stopped, and he spoke again: "Free my sister and choose this hand of flowers with which I forgive you, or choose the left and you and yours shall die this day." No sound was heard except the chirp of distant birds as all stood still in fear of what slaughter was to come. Slowly, oh, so slowly, came the Khan toward him, sword outdrawn. Each step as if he dragged a weight of stones, but finally face-to-face they stood, and still no sound. Then slowly, oh, so slowly, the Khan reached out and took the flowers. Such a sigh and murmur went throughout the crowd and some it is told fell upon their knees. The Khan now stepped aside and signaled for the girl's release.

She came on timid step to greet this unknown brother, unknown savior. But now he raised his left hand and offered her a garland of those self-same purple wildflowers which hand immediately before had held that darkened cudgel. No man could say how any of this took place, but who were there swore all their life that purple flowers came from out the air and the cudgel disappeared. And much more than that, the Khan was soon to relinquish all he had and take a hermit's garb, but first he made the new freed daughter a Queen over all his land.

His name was Besaga, and he stayed through the short summer, and visited with his sister often. He lived on the riverbank and spoke to all brave enough to approach. Many brought him food, which he gracefully accepted, but no offer of mead, no offer of wine was ever taken. Many children were given a small carving of an animal tooled by that stone knife, and many children were taught to braid garlands of wildflowers, both girls and boys. By and by, their fears allayed, many of the villagers came to sit with him on the stones at the riverbank. None have ever been found who could tell of what he said, but all professed that they were richer for their time with him, and even among them were some of the Khan's soldiers who had been there on that day.

With the first flake of snow, he told his sister farewell, and clasped the Khan in his giant arms, and up the mountain and into the trees he went. None felt it wise to follow. After some years, many of the children who had spent time with him began to search for him during the summer months, but no trace was ever found. Until this very day, there is not one soul in this village that does not believe that the great Besaga is still alive and traveling in some foreign land and still working his mysteries.

There follows, a long list of names, eighty-seven by count, which one must presume are those of the villagers who were present at that time. Following that is a somewhat longer list indicating descendants of those original persons, much like the listing in Genesis: "Mah-Sang begot Schoo, who begot Han, who begot Ari ben Dar." Which seem to indicate that this story had been handed down orally for some generations before a written version appeared. It also seems to me that names have changed from clearly Oriental to distinctly Arabic, which might support the footnote that it was first transcribed in Sumerian, even though the story strongly hints at a more Eastern origin.

Following, is what I believe to be a continuation, or at least another adventure of this same character. The document was translated from the Arabic, into Latin, and it again names the principal character in the other two pieces. This one I came across, myself, at the Library of Congress last summer. It is dated circa 825 A.D. It is quite short, and shows no authorship. Please see if you find the similarities that led me to believe that these two vastly separated stories have much in common, and indeed, must be about the same man.

He was tall, he was lean and his name was ibn Saga. He was tall as a camel and gaunt as a ghost. He walked into the oasis one day in the spring. None had seen him before. He wore but a simple, sleeveless toga with a snakeskin belt, and he slept on the open ground. He slept in the glens, he slept in the dunes, and he fasted four days of each week, and drank nothing but water from the spring. He was kind to the children and fashioned them playthings of straw, and never spoke to any man until spoken to first. After a time, Holy men came from afar and from near, and he talked to them long through the night. Wise men came from near and from far, and they listened to each word he said. A dog by his side as he went everywhere and he called to the dog, Be Gaz. And he walked out among the dunes early each day and only sometimes returned at night.

One hot autumn day a horde of Huns came down from the hills and settled in front of the spring. They exacted a fee from all who came to fill their jugs from the spring, and sooner or later, all had to come to survive. When ibn Saga came in from the dunes and found what had come to pass, he went to the Hun who was head of the pack and offered a simple choice. In one hand he held a fistful of seeds, in the other a large empty urn. "If you wish to stay, take these seeds and we will help you start a fine garden on the edge of this village; if you chose to go, you may fill this jug, and you will always have water at hand." The Hun drew his sword and stepped close to ibn Saga. Then he stopped short and asked, "We will always have water?" And ibn Saga answered, "As I have said."

In a very short time, the Hun had gathered his horde, filled the jug, and rode off, never to return. When the riders had left, ibn Saga filled his own jug with spring water, went to the outskirts of the village, dropped those seeds on the sandy ground and emptied his jug to water them. The next morning, he left the village, never to return, and by noon, three date trees and three olive trees had sprung from the ground he had watered.

I hope you can begin to see some connection not only in the actions of the character, but even, it seems to me in the manner of the storytelling. The following is the piece I found in the Fordham Library that started me on this strange journey. It was told to the monk and transcribed almost 350 years after the events described, and as I said, was originally in Latin.

From East he came astride a steed

    Of visage fearful, unknown of breed.

A mammoth head and eyes ablaze

    An alien soul in human shape.

From way beyond the Grecian isles

    Far beyond the Turks and Meads.

A savior sent to save this world?

    A scourge to drive the sinners down?

From East he came and caused alarms

    With frightful visage, bearing arms.

And with him came a dog called Guz,

With teeth like fangs in a monster's face,

For leagues they traveled, leagues and more

Nor food nor drink could stay their course

Nor river, wall nor mountain tall.

None opposed, so fierce their mien.

(Here, the rest of the page is missing, so we pick up on the next page.)

From East he came to the hills of Rome

And camping there he made his home.

He took his food from whom he chose

None dared challenge, no one would.

His face of stone would fright a Legion,

His dog a threat in every look,

Himself as large as two small men,

His shadow fell across the hills.

From East he came but with what cause?

What stopped him here? Why here to pause?

Rome saw fit to send out soldiers,

But none dared enter the alien's site.

Guards were posted to watch his moves

And Romans warned to be on guard.

But the terrible twosome was now settled in

A vacant villa was taken as home.

From East he came in summer's season.

In fall he showed some part of his reason.

The dog was sent with a note for the Pope;

He came unbridled and carried a message.

Guards took his missive and beat him away.

That, or no answer, was seen as a slight,

For twelve sheep were slaughtered and laid at Rome's gate,

One villa was torched and one olive grove hewn.

From East he came and his message was clear,

Besage was his name and his message is here:

'Melt your crosses, melt your chalices,

Sell your jewels and sell your books,

Open your palace, open your churches,

Good men are starving, children are dying,

Priests grow fat and bishops have fiefdoms,

"'Tis not why Peter came here to die?"

(Here the top of the page is missing, and it continues below.)

...   found no reply.

Now two dozen lambs lay dead at the gate,

A hillside of vines now trampled to dust.

High on the seventh hill of Rome

The twosome stood beside their home.

Below in all splendor rode in the Pope

'Mid six dozen Guards with lance and spear.

Up they rode to face the invaders,

Who dared to challenge his mighty realm

Was soon to meet the wrath of Rome,

The Vicar here of Christ on Earth.

Still he stood as made of stone

Against an empire, stood alone.

His left hand held a silver scimitar,

His right, a brightly blooming olive branch.

The Pope dismounted and faced his foe,

"Why came you here, barbarian fool?

How dare you challenge the Pope of Rome?

Begone, I command you, and come no more."

"I go where I must, be it even Hell's gate.

Comply with the message; there's no time to wait.

Take this branch, and give all to the poor,

Or next Sunday's mass will be said by another".

Swords were drawn at the end of these words,

Six dozen on one side, but none on the other.

"Take the branch, I beg you Papa,

Save your soul, save the Church to come."

The Pope returned under St. Peter's Dome,

Besage and his pair repaired to their home.

Two dozen more of the Palace Guard

Stayed in hope of containing those two.

Two olive branches not just the one,

Were seen by the wise men who counseled the Pope:

"Heed the warning that comes so strangely"

"Our God may work in mysterious ways."

Though some were well back from the scene of the pair,

All saw the same, all who were there.

As Besage stretched out his arms to the Pope,

There were two olive branches instead of just one.

The scimitar gone in the blink of an eye

And two offers of peace as clear as blue sky.

All who were there will always remember,

The miracle on the first of November.

John was the Pope and Sicco by name,

Powerful of family and a seeker of fame.

A Roman of stature and not to be swayed

Like many before, by hubris betrayed.

His orders were clear to "dispose of that giant,

'Fore next Sunday's Mass," but that was just rant,

For dawn found his body stone cold on that day,

And Besage and his troupe were long gone away.

I hope by now you see some of the connections that I made after my friend, Charlie Boyle, sent me that first piece. What later got my attention was that the final piece refers to an actual historical person in the naming of the Pope as Sicco because I found that was the name of

Pope John XVII. Below I have copied an extract from <u>The Catholic Encyclopedia.</u> The bold-face emphasis is mine:

"John XVII (XVIII), date of birth unknown; **d. November 6, 1003**. When Sylvester II died on May 12, 1003, there was no actual authority in Rome which could curb the nobles. Thus, the faction of Crescentius again won the upper hand, and John Crescentius, son of the patrician whom Otto III had defeated, seized the authority for himself. The three following popes were indebted to him for their elevation, and were made to feel his supremacy. A Roman, **Sicco, was first elected, and consecrated on June 13 as John XVII**, but died on November 6. Before taking orders. He had been married and had three sons who also became ecclesiastics. **Concerning his activities during the few months of his pontificate nothing has come down to us.**"

Furthermore, I call your attention to the line, in the next to last stanza above: "The miracle on the first of November." According to the Gregorian calendar, in the year 1003, the following Sunday would have been the sixth of November, the day of Sicco's actual death. For reasons unknowable, the storyteller wanted us to have that information, which seems to indicate that it was first told by an eye witness, or at least, someone very close to the event.

Allow me to recap here some of the similarities that I find inescapable: First, of course the name, which changes only slightly from Besaga, to bin Saga (ibn and bin both mean son of), to Besage; second, his height, which is compared to a bear, then a camel, and then to two small men; then there is the animal always with him: first a wolf and then a dog-like animal named BeGaz and then Guz. There is always a choice offered: cudgel or flowers, seeds or (perpetual?) water, olive branch or death, and, of course, there is always some version of a "miracle," or a "mystery." In the first two stories, the better choice seems to be made without any threat or coercion and all ends well. In the last re-telling, the proper choice is declined and death is the result. Not only that, but this is the last we ever hear of this character, and more than a thousand years have gone by.

If the first record of this event was indeed written in Sumerian, as the footnote suggests, then it must have occurred before the end of the first century A.D. because that language fell into total disuse after that time. The final story must have been carried orally for 300 to 350 years before it was recorded (1360AD), and the first one was not re-translated from the first century Sumerian for about 350 years (420AD). So, if we suppose the middle story was told for 300 to 350 years before it was written (825AD), then it might have occurred in the sixth century. It seems quite possible that this character could have re-appeared approximately every 400 or 500 years. If so – did we just miss the event in the dark ages of the sixteenth century? And is he going to appear again, on schedule, in the twenty-first?

Far-fetched, I admit, and built on the slimmest of extrapolations, but since the evidence is clear, that this tale, and this character, have turned up at somewhat regular intervals in times of crisis, and have, since the beginning of the Christian era, dare we not hope that this "Savior-Enigma" might somehow pay civilization another visit to help us through these extraordinarily precarious times?

I admit, your guess may be as good as mine. But there is always
Hope.

THE END

CHI-CHI

Cristen Carlos Gutierrez was born in Belize somewhere between twenty-eight and thirty years ago in the grubby, crime-ridden town of Orange Walk, where record keeping is little more than a hobby. His mother was a prostitute, as were many of the female population, and his father cannot be located in all of Central America. He is 5'10, weighs no more than 135 pounds, has a face covered with smallpox scars, jet black hair, and dirty-brown eyes. He seems always to have been called, "Chi-Chi," from his first recorded theft of a "case of cerveza" from the Lover's Bar, which is already a bit off the mark because the official language of Belize is English. His second reported crime was a "stabbing death," when he could have been no more than fourteen. The victim was apparently even a worse criminal, so the matter never went very far. The overall impression is that this is one skinny, ugly, mean son-of-a-gun.

There are no further mentions of him until he turns up in Los Angeles six years ago in the company of Dellasandro DeGama: a drug smuggler that I had chased before, and that's probably why Interpol posted me here to assist the LA Vice Squad. Sometimes our help in coordinating information on a criminal is essential in establishing a case; sometimes we are useful in apprehending the criminal; sometimes we merely confirm an identity. We at Interpol have no authority to arrest anyone unless they are considerate enough to commit a crime at our Headquarters in Lyon.

There are outstanding investigators in every country of the world; men of great intellect, extraordinary insight, and exceptional determination. What Interpol can sometimes bring to each case, besides extensive files on over twenty thousand miscreants from many countries, is an investigator who may have had first-hand contact with the culprit, may have picked up subtle bits of information that might never be included in a report. There are times when being on the scene will spark a memory of some tiny bit of evidence or some quirk of behavior that helps make that final connection to the criminal in question. In a sense, we are the "legs" of the local police force, and we have the resources to track a perpetrator across many borders and into foreign countries that they are seldom able to do.

I arrived in LA three nights ago, presented my bona fides to the tanned Desk Officer in the lobby of the unusual-looking building called Parker Center, which houses the LAPD Headquarters, picked up my hotel assignment, and got the first solid sleep I had in two days. I have a flat in Lyon, but I came here directly from Munich where, last night, I was assisting the local Bavarian authorities in arresting a con-artist who had eluded capture for over thirty years. The next morning, I reported to Captain Miles Prescott, head honcho in LA Vice, and the person I had been in communication with off and on over the last three years.

He looked to be in good shape, for a guy probably in his late fifties who sits behind a desk a lot. I knew him to be a straight-talker, and I soon found out that he was a very thoughtful and generous man as well. He had an accent that was strange to my ear, and I found out later that he was from Passaic, New Jersey. Believe me, they talk a distinctive patois. He introduced me to Detective Domingo (Dom) Sanchez with whom I would be working this case. Dom found me an empty desk in the squad room and helped me set up my computer and get organized. When I told him I wasn't comfortable in the hotel they put me in, he asked me a few questions about where I lived in Lyon, and then he booked me into this small hotel in Toluca Lake. I moved in last night, and so far, it feels like a perfect spot for me.

Interpol had no information on Chi-Chi, so I spent the rest of the day playing catch-up with the reports that Dom was sharing with me, because it looks as if Chi-Chi might be a central player in our investigation of DeGama.

About a year ago, I had tracked DeGama to Concepcion, in Honduras on the border with El Salvador. With a tip from an informer, I was able to direct the local Drug Enforcement Officers, the DGIC, to a warehouse where we engaged in gunfire with six men; two of whom were killed and three captured, but DeGama was not one of them. That concerned me a good deal because I had met an Officer at their Headquarters whom Interpol had on our "notices" as a former member of the notorious Battalion 3-16 "death squad," and men like that, in my experience, are never completely removed from criminal activities. I suspected that he has tipped DeGama off. The chances that I could run him down on his home turf again when he knew someone was after him seemed somewhere between slim and none, so I called Headquarters, told them my story, and they said, "Come on home." Words which I was happy to hear because I had been slogging through a half-dozen grubby little towns in El Salvador and Honduras for the last ten days before I got onto DeGama's trail, and I had enough of the heat, the humidity, and the stench to last me for quite a while. The places I had been staying, even the showers were filthy. I hopped a plane to San Pedro Sula, on the other side of Honduras, which was the closest international airport that could get me back to Lyon, and then – I got lucky.

There was a nice hotel at the airport where I got a hot shower and a decent night's sleep; I threw away most of my clothes, which were filthy, bought a shirt in the lobby, and changed into the cleanest pair of pants I had left. I was sitting at an island-shaped bar in the International Terminal, waiting for my three-thirty flight to Paris, when DeGama and five very grim guys who looked like they strangled cats for a hobby stomped in, pushed a couple of men aside, and occupied the other side of the island across from me. One of them was Chi-Chi, but I didn't know him at the time. The possibility of convincing the local security forces, who had no idea who I was, that this was a wanted man, and then getting them to quietly round up these six uglies without some kind of a blood bath in here – didn't seem like an idea that was worth acting on. I decided to stay with them as long as I could, call Lyon as soon as I got any workable information, and see if I could pick up any clues as to what was going on.

We sat there for almost forty minutes. What I saw was this: DeGama looked to be left-handed; he drank tequila shots like Russians drink vodka, often and quickly; his left eye blinked a lot, so it may have been impaired. Interpol had him at five foot eight, and I could tell that was a generous estimate; his upper torso looked like a body-builder's, muscles on top of muscles – do not go one-on-one with this bloke. My over-all impression was that if he was ordered to stop and put his hands up, his temperament would not allow him to do it. Much of this information may be totally useless, but it was in my memory bank and would soon be part of his Interpol file.

When they got up to leave, I called Lyon and told them what was up and for them to contact local Immigration here and find out where they were headed; I tried to cancel my flight (no dice), and said I planned to follow. It turned out that they were booked to Belem, in Brazil, a port town at the mouth of the Amazon, a thirteen or fourteen-hour flight from Honduras. What the hell were they up to? I really wanted to get on that plane with them, but Lyon said "no." First of all, there were six pairs of eyes that had probably registered me sitting across the bar from them; secondly, Belem was only sixteen hours from Paris, so they could have an agent in Belem within an hour or so of the gang's landing, and Immigration or local police would be warned to track them until he arrived, and thirdly, my Portuguese was pitiful on my best day. I got on the flight that they wouldn't let me cancel (lucky me), and headed home. The agent they sent to Belem lost DeGama and his pals the fourth day up the Amazon; no fault of his – the River is nearly 80 kilometers wide at its mouth; it's over 6,000 kilometers long, and it winds around like a drunken snake. But this was the back-story that convinced Lyon that when LA requested me, they had probably picked the right agent for the job. And so ... off to Southern California to pick up the trail of Dellasandro DeGama.

Six years ago, an unidentified body that OD'd on amphetamines, and had also been shot in the forehead post-mortem, turned up in a house that had been rented to Chi-Chi Guiterrez. When Homicide picked him up, he was with DeGama in a bar in Compton, and that's when Vice got interested. Both of them had alibis for the time of death, confirmed by three Hispanics (all of whom had a record) and the bartender, but Vice started keeping tabs on them and reported to us in Lyon because DeGama was on "notice." Since then, DeGama, and often Chi-Chi, visited either El Salvador or Honduras about once every six months. When they returned to LA, there was regularly a noticeable bump up in the amount of cocaine available on the streets of LA, but so far, no way of connecting them to any shipments. As was to be expected, neither the Salvadorian nor the Honduran Police had any information on the movement of any drugs.

Two years ago, when Captain Prescott and I were trading emails, he was bemoaning the fact that he had this obvious drug-dealer right in front of him, but nobody could nail him with anything. As a joke, I reminded him that one of his countrymen had a similar problem with Al Capone, and maybe he should get the Treasury Department involved. Much to my surprise, he did, and it turned out that DeGama had never filed an Income Tax Return, so Prescott assigned Dom Sanchez to track as many of DeGama's purchases and spending habits as he could find. That was a long and tedious process. The day before Prescott called Lyon to get me over here, Chi-Chi Gutierrez applied for a loan to buy a large, old house in the Hollywood Hills above Sunset Blvd. and a check for $110,000, drawn on a bank in Honduras, signed by DeGama, was being held in escrow. If this check was cashed, they had proof positive that DeGama was guilty of Income Tax evasion. Not the ideal ending for a drug smuggler's capture, but a damn good start and maybe, a lot of leverage to get DeGama to trade his supply routes and entry points for a few years off the sentence.

I got the idea that the only reason Prescott called for me was because I had given him the idea for this, and he wanted me to be in on the collar and give me a trip to sunny Southern California as a reward. I felt obligated to call Lyon and tell them that LA wanted me to stick around, but I honestly didn't have a lot to do. They told me to hold, and after about two minutes, Ivan Bogdonavitch got on the line and told me he'd get back to me and meantime, "Just soak up a lot of sun." Ivan is a Paris-born Jew who speaks seven or more languages, runs the North American desk and has a really wry sense of humor. I just knew he had checked the weather in LA before he made the call because it was raining torrents today in "sunny Southern California." I asked Dom what he thought I should do, and he suggested I call him each morning and again about five in the afternoon and he could keep me updated; then he gave me a beeper in case I ever got out of cell range and told me to, "Go have some fun." Sounded good to me, so the next thing I did was call Ginny Downs, the attractive young lady that I had questioned in Vienna, flew from Munich with, and had a lengthy conversation with on our flight to LA.

Ginny

Alright – what the heck is wrong with me? I just had the worst experience of my life; I was questioned by police and held in custody; I was a "person of interest" in some terrible crime, and all of this because I let some older man talk me into taking a trip to Europe with him. Not only that, but he was a criminal of some kind, and I had no idea about that. Not a clue. Was I blind, or just stupid, or both? And now here's this other guy, who must be more than ten years older than me, he's got to be in his late thirties or early forties, and here I am, after just four or five hours of talking to him on a plane, and I can't stand it that he hasn't called me yet. I don't know, maybe it's like Phyllis and Astrid said. When I told them all about my "vacation to hell" and the Detective that I stayed up all night talking to on the plane, they both said that I was probably looking for a "Father figure." Well I don't think so. First of all, neither one of these men looks anything like my father, and secondly my father was born in California and I don't think he ever left it, and these two guys both had sort of been all over the world. Besides, I got along fine with my father right up to the day he and Mom were killed in that car crash. "Father Figure" – no, I don't think so.

But *something* is going on with me because I spent most of yesterday trying to make a list of places in LA that I would like to show him. You know, I figured he had been like "everywhere," but I bet he never saw anything like the LaBrea Tar Pits; that's got to be something special. And then Venice Beach; everybody says there is nothing, anywhere, like the Boardwalk there with the jugglers and skate-boarders and novelty shops and all that, and what about driving from the Ocean up to Angeles Crest Highway and being in snow up the wazoo in less than an hour. I bet you can't do that in any of those places he's been. It's April, there must be snow up there now. Then, for something romantic I thought of this Japanese restaurant in Hollywood that sits way up on top of a hill where you can see almost the whole city spread out in front of you. I'm not crazy about raw fish and all that, but if you're there at just about sundown, when the lights are going on all over the city, it's really something. I don't see how he could not like that.

Just before I got ready for bed, I started planning my wardrobe. I mean … really? But I did. I thought of these neat cream-colored shorts I have and that navy-blue blouse that fits me really, really well, and that would be great for Venice Beach. Then I realized that it's still chilly, and I'd have to wear some kind of jacket over the blouse, but then I thought, no, that would be even better, because he could spend the first part of the day looking at my legs and then, if we went to lunch or something, I could peel off the jacket and I would have some … "other things" for him to look at. Yeah, that could be okay. Then I started thinking about the Japanese place, and I knew I wanted something sexy but demure and dressy, but definitely a dress, so that would have to be Phyllis. I have lots of blouses and skirts because that's what they want you to wear at work, but I don't buy a lot of dresses. Phyllis does – I guess because she always goes to work in slacks and tee shirts; she's a dental assistant, and she wears a lab coat or something at work. So, I went through her stuff this morning, and I think I've settled on this dark crimson, low cut number that I borrowed once before and got a lot of attention. I don't think it's too obvious, but I'll ask Phyllis before I decide for sure.

Now, here I sit, all by myself … Phyllis is out for the evening … and why doesn't the damn phone ring! I've got two more days of vacation time before I have to go back to work, because my lovely vacation was cut short by this police thing, and I just wanted to get home as soon as I could after it was all over. He and I both got back here on the same plane, and it's two days later … and he hasn't called … and it's beginning to piss me off! I mean … I didn't ask him – he said he would call as soon as he got checked in with his new "assignment." All hush, hush, of course; he wouldn't tell me anything about that. Big deal with all his international police work and "Interpol," whatever that is … but the trouble is … the trouble is … I just want to hear his voice again. He's got this little teeny, tiny hint of an Irish brogue with some of his words, and it just makes me go all giggly. I mean … how silly is that? I'm twenty-six, I'm not sixteen, but when he talked to me in that soft, almost a whisper voice, I just got all Jell-O inside. Damn girl … get a hold of yourself!

When the phone rang, I jumped a foot! It was him - it was the Irishman, and he apologized for not calling sooner, but he said something unusual had developed, which might be nice for both of us, if I was still interested in seeing him, because it looked as if he might have a couple days off and maybe we could spend some time together. I managed not to scream, "Yes!" and told him that I was sure I could work something out to be able to see him, and he seemed very, very pleased to hear that. He said he knew it was late tonight … it was nine o'clock? … that was "late" for him? … but he would rent a car and pick me up whenever I was free tomorrow, and I could show him around LA. I told him not to bother renting a car; I would pick him up tomorrow in my hot little eight-year-old Miata. "Just tell me where you are and what time you want to start." He gave me the address of his hotel in Toluca Lake and suggested that we have a late breakfast at this little outdoor coffee place a few blocks from his place about ten … if it wasn't raining. It took us a couple minutes to get through a bunch of awkward "good-nights" and "good-byes", and as soon as he hung up, I threw myself on my bed and pounded the devil out of my pillow and rolled over on my back and laughed out loud. Yes – this was going to be good! … this was going to be VERY good!

I went to the kitchen and poured myself a big glass of red wine – I don't kid myself, I can't tell one of them from another, so I buy Gallo because it comes in a big jug and it's cheap. And I thought, "Well, it's 'late' for him so why don't I just go to bed." On my way to sleep, I decided I'd take him to Venice Beach tomorrow and hit him with the shorts and sexy blouse; give him both barrels and see what that did for him. Yes – this was going to be *gooooood*.

I wasn't sure what I was getting into, but then, whoever is "sure"? This was a really cute young girl – but there you go, "young;" what the hell was I thinking? I'm forty-one, she's in her mid-to-late twenties, and already I knew we were from totally different worlds. However – she was a hoot to listen to and bright as a new penny. But what did I know? Twelve years ago, I met a woman who was five years older than me, and fell totally in love for the first, and so far, only time in my life. Who can tell anything about love?

Her name was Christine, Christine St. Albans, and she ran this little Bakery-Coffee Shop a couple of blocks from my first flat in Lyon when I was doing my basic training. I used to eat breakfast there almost every morning, and after three weeks or so, she came and sat at my table and said, "OK, Copper, spill the beans."

Well, that blew me away! She somehow knew I was a policeman, and she had picked up this expression from some gangster movie she must have seen. She was smart, smarter than me; she was funny as the dickens and blessed with that wonderful French pragmatism that sees the world exactly as it is, and deals with it. This was some hip Mademoiselle! But she wasn't exactly that either – she was a "Madame," because she had been married and divorced before she was twenty-five.

She was also a knockout. At work she kept a kerchief on her hair, wore no make-up, and worked in a shapeless smock. The first time we went out, she bowled me over: she had long dark brown hair, a beautiful figure, cheekbones that I had somehow never noticed and her greenish eyes were as brilliant as the hills of Kilkenny.

We talked every morning after that and saw each other in the evenings when I had one of my few nights away from the training. After about six months I moved into her flat over the Bakery, and for the next three years I was as happy as I have ever been, before or since. Why I didn't ask her to marry me, God only knows, but it would probably have still ended up the same as it did anyway. We loved without any reservations that I was aware of, and she said it broke her heart to send me away. It certainly broke mine.

After I finished the training, I began getting postings to mostly English-speaking locations, because my other language skills were still only what the instructors called "passable." Christine seemed to adjust very easily to me being gone for days or sometimes weeks at a time. Coming home was always a time that seemed to sharpen our need for each other, but three years on, after I got shot in Amsterdam, and they brought me back to the hospital in Lyon to recuperate, things changed.

She came to see me in hospital and sat with me for hours, and we had a cot brought in so she could stay the night. But when it was time for my release, she told me that she couldn't take it; she couldn't live with the thought that I might go away some day, and never come back. She saw us living our lives together and could even accept our dying together, but not apart … not one of us alone … not me in some strange place without her. She said that she couldn't bear to see me again, knowing we could never be together … that was too hard. She had my things moved back to the flat I had kept. I never went to her shop again; I never saw her again. The next few months were the worst time of my life. The pain has become less acute, but it's there. It's always there, in the back.

After a while, I saw that life was going on, with or without me, so I decided to get back on the boat and ride down the river wherever it took me. I've always enjoyed the company of women, and I've had a lot of good times, but when there seems to be a serious attraction, I have always been careful to present my job, my devotion to it, and the life it demands as clearly as I can – and I have noticed that the temperature drops a few degrees almost instantly. But what am I supposed to do? Here I am, a healthy guy, in what many think of as the prime of life, with an off-putting career and a hankering for female companionship. So, I just keep dipping my oar in the water, and keep hoping. What the hell – I'm a lucky guy, right?

Ginny

Well, the last two days have been even better than I had hoped for – dammit, and now what do I do? He couldn't take his eyes off me from the very first second he saw me in the front seat of my Miata. The cream-colored shorts were the perfect choice, and after we had breakfast, I drove us out to Venice Beach and he kept shaking his head and grinning and pointing to all the weirdos. I was right, he had never seen any place quite like it, and we had lunch right on the Boardwalk and after, he wanted to stay and just watch the jugglers, and the weight-lifters and the pan-handlers. Before lunch, I put my hand through his arm as we walked along and after lunch, he took my hand and held it wherever we went for the rest of the day. When I peeled off my jacket and he got a load of me in that tight blouse, well … that may have had something to do with it. Whatever … it was a terrific start.

After we had dinner at an Italian place on Venice Boulevard on the way back, I asked him if he wanted to stop by my place for a nightcap, but he said he would feel more comfortable at the place where the LA Police had booked him. When I got him to Toluca Lake, we had four really sweet kisses, and he told me what a great time he had and he hoped we could start tomorrow the same way. That was all fine and good, but he never mentioned, "Do you want to come up for a drink," or anything, so I was left kind of wondering, was it him or was it me? I had to give the day a B plus and started thinking about how I could get an A tomorrow.

After we had breakfast the next morning, I took him to the Tar Pits, and he was really impressed; he got a bunch of the literature and sat on a bench to read about it. I had to wonder if my choice of jeans and a pink off-the-shoulder blouse was not hot enough to keep him focused on me. But as soon as he read a portion of it, he kind of jumped up and gave me a big hug and a quick kiss and told me I was "terrific," and what a "brilliant idea" it was to choose this place. I figured, Angeles Crest would be another place he would love, and maybe I would get another kiss – but he asked me how far it was, and when I told him, he said he'd rather just sit with me and talk. I liked *that* idea. He asked if I liked wine and cheese and picnics, and when I said okay, he had me take him to a "nice" store, which I figured was Pavilions. He got three different cheeses and two bottles of wine and some dark bread, and off we went to Griffith Park, where there are lots of picnic tables and grass to sit on and greenery and miles and miles of walking trails.

I can't remember what all we talked about, but a lot of it was silliness; some of it was movies that we liked, stories about our parents, about our friends, what made us laugh, and a little bit about what we did for a living. What he did excited him, but it scared me, maybe because I couldn't see me in that part of his life at all. I don't think he noticed that, but we talked until the light began to fade, and I felt we were as close to each other as any two people have been that soon. We wrapped up what was left of the bread and cheese and took the unopened bottle of wine and went to his hotel.

For a tough looking guy, he was just so tender and gentle. I don't know that it was the best sex I ever had, but there was something about his strength and sureness that left me feeling that I had never been loved by anyone quite like that. We got up and showered together and had a little more of the wine and the bread and the cheese. We didn't talk much; I don't think we needed to, and we went back to bed, and I slept in his arms all night. Until his phone woke us the next morning and took him away from me ... maybe forever.

We were a small caravan winding up these narrow streets in the hills above Sunset Boulevard: a squad car in front and back with two Uniforms in each, then Dom and me, and then two Treasuries in another car. We stopped in front of Chi-Chi's soon-to-be new home and met another Vice Detective named Carter, who had reported them being here. Two of the Uniforms re-routed traffic around the scene and the other two were dispatched to watch the sides of the house, because the hill dropped away at about a sixty-degree angle and the house sticks out in the air with nothing but long, slender poles to keep it from falling down. There was no other way of observing the back. Dom knocked loudly, announced "Police" and then we all pushed past Chi-Chi and entered this large room where one wall was nothing but glass, overlooking half the city. We had two warrants, one to search the premises and one for the arrest of Dellasandro DeGama on violation of Income Tax reporting.

Chi-Chi was seriously pissed and insisted that DeGama was not here. Dom and one of the T-Men went to check out the upstairs and Carter and the other T-Man went to check out the lower level; I was left to babysit Chi-Chi, who almost had steam coming out of his ears. After a couple of minutes of heavy-footed stomping around the room, Chi-Chi said he wanted a glass of water and was going into the kitchen. It's been over ten years since I trusted *anything* that a suspect told me, and that trust got me a bullet in the chest, so I seldom do that anymore. I pulled my .38 from my holster and carried it by my side and followed Chi-Chi into the kitchen.

I carry a small, light, Smith & Wesson .38 Airweight, and although I regularly qualify on it, I have only fired it in action less than a half dozen times: a year ago in Honduras, which was a major mismanagement of a collar, and I'm not sure I even hit anybody there; twice I shot a fleeing subject, once in Dublin and once in Cairo. But I've never really shot to kill anyone.

I had just entered the doorway when Chi-Chi wheeled around and swung at me with a long-blade kitchen knife. I threw up my left hand and caught a huge, deep slice through my palm, and then I shot him twice in the chest. Chi-Chi didn't fall down – he just stood there with this look of total surprise on his face. Apparently, no one in Belize had ever told him that you don't bring a knife to a gunfight; then he fell over, flat on his back. Barely a second later, I heard breaking glass and then shouts about, "He's running," and "Down the hill."

The two Uniforms had already started sliding down the hill after DeGama as Dom and the T-man came tearing down the stairs, ran outside, and joined the chase. I went to the glass doors and stepped out on the balcony to watch. There were four of them after him, all sliding down the hill on their butts and trying to maintain their balance. DeGama got as far as a six-foot retaining wall that separated the next property down the hill, and when Dom and the T-Man yelled at him to stop, he made the mistake of turning around and pulling his gun. The four lawmen in pursuit must have put ten shots in him in about three seconds. And that was that.

Now that it seemed to be over, I noticed that I had been dripping a lot of blood across this expanse of beige carpet and that I was feeling a bit light-headed. I sat down on the floor and waited for the guys to get back. Dom had to slap my face to wake me, so I must have passed out; he had called for the EMTs and asked me if I was a "woos," (whatever the hell that was), and he wrapped a kitchen towel around my hand. Meanwhile, Carter and the T-Man had found nearly a kilo of coke in the downstairs refrigerator, and a couple of minutes later the place was a mob scene; police cars and TV helicopters and mobile news vans and two Coroner's vans and a pair of "Suits" from Internal Affairs and a big, tall, skinny guy from Homicide who took charge. Fortunately, the EMTs arrived, bandaged my hand, and one of them told the Homicide guy that I had to get this hand treated or I was going to lose it. I gave "Homicide" a brief version of the events that led to Chi-Chi's death, handed over my weapon, and he cleared me to leave. Dom had to stay on the scene, but he told a Uniform named Perkins to take me to "Cedars," and I was out of there.

Cedars Sinai is a big, busy hospital, but the Emergency Room went totally quiet when Perkins led me in there and yelled, "Officer wounded here!" Two doctors and two nurses were on me in a second. The next few minutes were a bit of a blur; I know they gave me a shot in the arm, and I know they called a surgeon down from somewhere upstairs, and I know he gave me another shot in my hand, and then it got really fuzzy. When I woke up, I was propped up on a gurney, my hand was in a huge bandage, and it stung like hell. I had an IV in my arm and Perkins was sitting in a chair next to me with a cup of coffee and – I had to laugh at the cliché – a doughnut.

I wanted to find out if and when I could get out of here, so I pushed the call-button and almost before I took my thumb off it, there was a nurse and an intern at the foot of my bed. I asked them what the story was, and the nurse said she would get "Doctor something-something" and she was off like a shot. The Intern told me that Dr. Kleinmetz (that was his name) was one of the top reconstruction surgeons on the West Coast, and I was probably going to be "just fine," and asked if he could get me anything. I allowed as how a cup of strong tea with milk and sugar and, of course, "a doughnut" would be just fine. He laughed and said he would see what he could do. About five minutes later, he trailed Dr. Kleinmetz into the room and gave me a cup of tea and my doughnut.

Kleinmetz told me that I had lost a serious amount of blood, but I was "a lucky young fella," and proceeded to explain how lucky: the knife had only severed the tendons to the last two fingers on my hand, and he had joined them back well enough that, in time, they could be partially useful. Also, he said, if anyone had cut that deeply into my fingers instead of my hand, it would have been a very lengthy and tricky reconstruction to ever get them re-attached and in working order. I think that was meant to cheer me up. Since then, every time I try to grab something in my left hand, I remember Chi-Chi.

Ginny

When Patrick answered that phone call this morning, it was a few minutes after eight, and in less than fifteen minutes, he was gone. I think his head was out of there from the second he picked it up; I talked to him while he was dressing and strapping an empty holster on (I didn't notice that last night), but he didn't seem to hear me, (and he certainly wasn't seeing me) and only responded with a grunt here and there. I grabbed a towel to cover myself and followed him around and managed to kiss him on the cheek before he was out the door, but I don't think any of that registered with him. He didn't even say, "I'll call you."

I got dressed and wandered around his hotel room, trying to get more of an idea what he was like; the usual socks and boxers, shirts, one pair of slacks and a dark suit – nothing. So, I came home, fixed breakfast and watched some TV; fixed lunch and watched some TV, and now I'm warming a Tilapia TV dinner and still watching the damn TV and it's now almost eight p.m. Has he left town? Is he dead? Has he completely forgotten about me? If this is how it would be with him, maybe I'm better off if he never calls again.

No – that's a terrible idea; I want to see him so bad I can't stand it, and if this is what my life would be like if we were together, I honestly don't know if I could stand that either, but I know I would like to try. Oh, girl – what have you got yourself into now? I think I'll drink about a quart of wine and try to calm down.

Phyllis came home, and as soon as she walked in, I burst into tears and sobbed out the whole fantastic story of yesterday and the god-awful story of today. She's great! She turned off the TV and fed me Kleenex and held me and let me ramble on until I just didn't have anything else to say; then poured us both a big glass of wine, propped our feet up on the coffee table and put her arm around me. It was then nine o'clock and at ten after, the phone rang. It was him.

He apologized for not calling me earlier, but he said something unforeseen had happened and he knew it was late … it was nine o'clock, again? … and I was beginning to get one of those Deja-vu things … but this time he asked if he could come over. I said, "Come." I dried my eyes, scrubbed my face, put on fresh make-up, grabbed my favorite tee shirt and my tightest jeans. Phyllis said she could go to her room or stay with me, I said, "Go." She put a bottle of her wine, a Pinot Noir, on the table with two clean glasses and said, "Just in case he likes real wine," kissed me on top of my head, and closed her door. I don't know where he was when he called, but it couldn't have been more than ten minutes before our intercom pinged, and I heard his crinkly voice say "Michael, here." I buzzed him in, and while I was waiting for him to climb the stairs, I told myself three things: you're a grownup, you're a lady, and you are not to jump his bones as soon as he comes through the door.

When I opened the door, I froze; he was deathly pale, and he looked like he was in pain with this big bandage on his hand. The fingers that were sticking out were all purplish and blue. He said, "Sorry ... can I come in?"

I took his other hand and led him over to the sofa; he said, "Sorry," again and then slowly told me what had happened today. When he finished, I went into his arms and held on for dear life; my God! ... he could have been killed today! Then I started blubbering, and instead of me comforting my poor wounded hero, here he was taking care of me.

We talked – well, mostly he talked, and I mostly listened, until past midnight; mostly about how this was his life for the foreseeable future, and how difficult this would be for any woman to live with, and how he needed to leave that decision in my hands. Heavy stuff. We slept together, but no love-making, but I wanted to be naked next to him, and when he held me, I could tell he really liked that.

When we got up the next morning, Phyllis was already gone, and I fixed us some scrambled eggs and rooted around for some tea for him instead of coffee. We both showered, but not together this time, and I took him down to the Police Headquarters for him to get his gear, pick up his gun, and say his goodbyes. He was booked on a three-thirty flight to Lyon. He introduced me to a police Captain and another detective named Dom; there was a lot of guy hugs and back slapping and a couple of warnings about "… try not to cut yourself when you're shaving," … which I didn't get, and then I took him to his hotel to pack. We had about an hour to kill before we had to be at LAX, and he took us over to a nearby bar called Timmy Nolan's and ordered us both a "pint of Guinness." Well… it wasn't nearly as bad as that stuff I drank in Prague a week or so ago, but it was pretty bitter; he finished mine, and we were off to LAX. What is it with men and terrible tasting beer?

I dropped him off at the International Terminal, and we held each other for a few precious moments, and then we had a long, lingering kiss, and he turned and walked away. Is that the end of my unbelievable "adventure?"

I like Business Class. The seats are decent, and the service is good, and you don't feel as if you are throwing money away on First Class. Of course, it's not really "my" money; on flights over five hours, Interpol always books us in Business, and I'm happy with that policy. I'm sipping a dram of Jameson, maybe halfway across this huge country and headed back to Lyon for a week of desk service. They told me that I was not going into the field again until our doctors gave me a clean bill of health. I know I'll get itchy feet after a couple of days, but right now, that desk sounds just fine.

I think I did right by Ginny – I hope so. Even though it was only a few days, I felt like I was close to falling in love, and I think she was, too. What I learned from Christine was, that you have to see things through your lover's eyes, and all I could see for Ginny was a long-distance relationship filled with a lot of loneliness and worry and frustration, because I knew that I was going to be doing this job until something or someone stopped me. That didn't seem fair to her, so I tried to dissuade her from hanging on to this new "us" she had discovered, and move on with her life.

I knew she might be hurting or confused and that's why I wanted to spend our last night together, and I didn't want us to make love again because that would just make the parting worse, but when she decided to get into bed naked ... Jesus, Mary, and Joseph! ... all my good intentions almost went up in smoke. Almost. She is wonderful! I know I was captivated by her; she's unique – she's a fresh, bright, open soul – whom I would surely like to be with, but in all fairness, I think I need to leave that choice in her hands.

I will always remember Ginny ... and, I will always remember Chi-Chi – the first man I ever killed.

THE END

THE KEY

She had given me the key so she knew I was coming, but I still wanted to surprise her. Now that I was in her apartment, I was having second thoughts; I didn't want to frighten her. Maybe I should just go back outside and call her … no, the hell with it … don't be such a "country boy."

I put the cream cheese and lox in the fridge, the bagels on the counter, took off my jacket and dropped it in the living room and eased up to her bedroom door. I pushed it open little by little, and looked in. It was really dark. She told me that she has these "blackout" curtains on both windows because her bedroom gets the morning sun and it was waking her up when she first moved in here. I could just barely make out her form under the covers; on her side and slightly curled up with just her left shoulder peeking out. God, she is so pretty! I just watched her sleep for a few minutes, thinking I was one lucky son-of-a-gun to be hanging out with a woman as terrific as this.

Yeah, but … I really hadn't thought this thing through … What do I do now? I didn't want to scare her, and I didn't want to stand there like some Peeping Tom, just watching until she woke up. So, I reached down and brushed a few strands of hair off her face and kissed her real lightly on the cheek. She moved ever-so-slightly and I heard a tiny sound, like "mmmmmmmmm." But then, nothing more. Then I put my hand very lightly on her hip like you would to wake a small child, and left it there, and after about a minute she wiggled her fanny a bit and curled up into a tighter position, and I heard another "nnnnnnnnng," but she had pushed some of the covers off of her and I could see that she was wearing this flimsy sort of top and the strap had fallen off her shoulder. So I leaned down and very gently kissed her bare shoulder, and that must have gotten through to her consciousness because she slowly rolled over on her back, and with her eyes still closed, she reached her arms up to me, and so I sat on the edge of her bed and leaned in and she wrapped her arms around me, pulled me closer, snuggled her face into my neck and said, "mmmmmmmmm."

"How about getting up, Sleepy Head?"

"Nuh Uh."

"Is that a 'No'?"

"Uuuuuh!"

"Aren't we going to the beach, today ... don't you want to go early?"

"Nnnnnnnnnnnuh!"

"Okay ... I brought bagels and lox, so I'm going into the kitchen and start fixing them, and then I'm going to start eating them, and if you want any, you're going to have get out there before I finish them."

Then she pushed me away and said, "You're mean!" But she left her hands on my chest and then slowly moved them up to my face and pulled me down again and kissed me ... kissed me so softly; then she pushed me away again and said, "Get out! I've got to get dressed," and I got up off the bed and put my hand on her beautiful, soft cheek ... and just looked at her ... and then I left.

I got some plates out of the cabinet and set out the cream cheese and the lox, and then found a bread knife and split two of the bagels, a sesame for her and a plain for me, and rooted around and found the coffee and measured out four cups and got that going and found two cups and the Sugar In The Raw. I set the table and sat down to wait for her and for the coffee. As I looked out the window, I started wondering just how the hell this grocery clerk from Brentwood, Tennessee came to be sitting in this beautiful girl's apartment in the middle of Los Angeles, CA.

I guess, to be accurate, I'm not just a grocery clerk, but that's how I've thought of myself for most of my life because I grew up in my mom and dad's grocery store, and it wasn't until later that I started to manage it and started doing this writing thing. Mom and Dad have this little store in Brentwood, which is a suburb of Nashville, and we lived behind the store, out near Apple Lake, until I was twelve and Dad expanded the store and bought a new house that was only two blocks away. I worked in the store with them since I was six and all through high school; after school and weekends. My dad insisted that I should have "the college experience," which to him meant living in a dorm and just coming home for holidays, even though I was going to Tennessee State, which is right here in Nashville. I did that until Mom's knees gave out about the end of my sophomore year and then I came back to live at home and sort of take on a little more responsibility.

Over the next few years, Logan Appleby and I helped Dad manage the store, and about six years ago, Dad's arthritis kind of caught up with him, and although he always liked going down to market every morning, now he only comes in three or four mornings a week, and Mom walks the aisles and sits up front and chats with our customers two or three days each week. There has always been a lot of pressure from all the big grocery chains to sell out, but Mom and Dad had a lot going for them because of two things that that they did early on. Dad grew up on a farm, and he knew practically every grower there was all the way down to Shelbyville, and he knew good produce when he saw it and was willing to pay for the best, so even if our customers might be paying a bit more, they knew it was always going to be the best grown around here. The second thing was a piece of bad luck-good luck when Dad heard about this baker, Fritz Stovall, over in Antioch, who had to give up his bakery because they were going to tear the building down; that's when Dad turned our living quarters into a bakery, and that's when we moved to a real house. We had breads and pastries and pies and cakes, all fresh-made right in our store, long before any of the chains started doing that.

Shortly after Logan and I started running the store, I moved into a little cabin over on Sevenmile Creek and I also started taking some classes up at Vanderbilt on a couple of evenings. In this English class, the professor gave us an assignment to write about our heritage, so I started thinking about my dad's people who came through the Cumberland Pass with Daniel Boone – or so the family story goes, and I decided to write to Uncle Birch, who is really Dad's uncle and the oldest person in our family. He was eighty-seven then, and he wrote me back a six-page, legal-size yellow tablet full of stuff about his grandfather, William Calloway, whose mother was Jemima Boone, Daniel Boone's brother's daughter. (You following that?) So, for class I wrote a story about that and later, Uncle Birch and I started writing back and forth, and he started telling me stories about growing up in Tennessee, and that's how I got interested in writing short stories about rural life around home.

In about a year, I had twelve short stories, all set in Tennessee about some people that I actually knew, some that Uncle Birch told me about, and mostly about rural folks from days gone by that I made up, and I showed them to a teacher up at Vanderbilt and this English professor edited them for me and encouraged me to print copies and send them to some Publishers. With his help, I did; under the title of "Tales from Tennessee." About six months later I got this letter from John Hargrove of Spencer-Hargrove Publishing in New York saying how much he liked "Tales" and asking if I had anything else to show him. Well, I didn't, but he offered to fly me up there for a couple of days that fall to meet some people, because he wanted to publish the short stories!

This was really unexpected because I was just sort of writing to amuse myself and any folks around the store who wanted to read these yarns, but that fall I went up and attended four or five cocktail parties and signed a lot of books at the Ninety-Second Street Y and had a long talk with Mr. Hargrove who wanted me to write a novel, because apparently short stories are hard to sell and don't make much money. I say, "apparently," because the biggest check I ever got from "Tales," was Three Hundred and Eighty-Six dollars, and that was the only one ever, over three hundred. So, I thought I'd give it a try, and I set myself the task of finding something that I cared about that could maybe take up more than twenty or thirty pages, and Uncle Birch was the one who gave me the idea. Here's what we came up with: try to track down the descendants of the forty families that originally came through the Cumberland Gap into Tennessee and Kentucky with Daniel Boone and try to follow the accomplishments or the problems of one of these pioneer families.

Well, that seemed like a great idea at the time, but after about six months of doing research into birth and death records and trying to track people who started out living in a wilderness, I realized that I didn't have the patience for honest-to-goodness research; so what I did was I changed some of the names a little and made up stories about ten families who were early settlers around here and then created tales about their (supposedly) most interesting descendant. So there were some stories about the early 1800's and some about the late 1800's and others on up to about 1950, and I called it "Boone's Legacy," and Hargrove published it and, although it never appeared on the NY Times Best Seller List, two clubs had it on their "Book Of The Month" list and I've been getting nice size checks for the past year. Hargrove and I were equally aware that I had not really written a novel, and we both felt that we were pretty lucky that we had actually managed to get another bunch of short stories published under slightly false pretenses. I figured this was probably the last time I would be involved with the world of publishing. But that was not quite the end of "Boone's Legacy."

Last month, a fellow named Morton Culbertson calls me out of the blue from Warner Bros. Studios, in Los Angeles, and tells me he wants me to come spend a week with some of his writers to turn "Boone's Legacy" into a feature film. It turns out that he is the new Director of Development on the Warner Bros. Lot, and although I told him at the time that I didn't think my book was movie material and also that I knew nothing about writing screen plays, he had already sent a check to Hargrove for Fifty Thousand Dollars for the film and ancillary rights, had booked an apartment for me, right across from the Lot in Burbank and would have my first class ticket waiting at Nashville International as soon as I said yes. Well, Mom and Dad thought it was wonderful, and Logan said he could handle the store for a couple of weeks easy, so I closed up the cabin, packed a bag and my original manuscript of the "Legacy" and … "California, Here I Come."

———————————

When I got off the plane, there was a driver waiting for me, and he took me over to this big, sprawling apartment complex right across from the Warner Bros. lot and told me that as soon as I could get settled, he was to take me to dinner to meet the two writers I was going to be working with. He dropped me at the Registration Center and said he would wait for me. I went up to the Desk and this young woman came around the counter and said, "I love 'The Boone Legacy,' I think you're brilliant Mr. McCabe, and I want to play Rebecca Bryan … here's my picture and resume," and she handed me a large grey envelope, picked up a set of keys, grabbed my other hand and started walking us out the door, saying, "I'll show you to your unit, and then I'll take you to dinner, and we can talk about it. I have a couple of really neat ideas … and you'll be surprised how much Rebecca and I are alike."

By this time, we were almost to the car, and my driver stepped in front of her and said, "Can I help you Mr. McCabe?" Surprisingly she stopped talking for a second and I had time to say: "Thank you, Miss, but I'm afraid I already have dinner plans, so if you could just give me my keys …?"

"Oh … okay, sure … (she did) … and call me when you get back …
it doesn't matter how late, okay?"

"Well, we'll see … thank you."

"Oh sure … and don't forget … Libby Shaw … okay?"

"I couldn't possibly." And we drove off.

That was how I met Libby Shaw.

The apartment was very nice and about the size of my whole cabin. I
washed up and changed clothes; the driver said we had plenty of time, so
when I was ready, he took us over to a very nice place called Le Petit
Chateau. As soon as I came in, this gentleman said, "Mr. McCabe?" and
when I nodded, he took me over to meet the two gentlemen I would be
spending the next week with: Doug Saunders and Clay Dunham. (How
did he know who I was? Did I have hayseed in my hair?) Doug was
about my height, just a bit heavier, with dark brown hair, brown eyes,
and a very nice tan; also, a good handshake; Clay was of smaller stature,
almost fragile looking, also brown haired and brown-eyed and an extra
firm handshake. Both looked to be in their mid-forties. Doug was
drinking a vodka martini, and Clay said he was drinking something called
"Kir." When I looked quizzical, he said, "Oh, it's made with Cassis,"
which didn't help me at all; I had a Jack Daniels with a little water and sat
back to find out how these miracle men were going to turn this rambling
tale of mine into a motion picture script. All I heard for the next hour or
so was how much they loved the Legacy and how charming the "Tales"
were and how fascinating it was that my characters really lived in
Tennessee. When I broached the subject of actual "writing" they
skittered away to another topic as if I had used a cuss word in church.
We were to get together tomorrow afternoon "about two-ish" to make

some plans to start tackling the "treatment," as they called it, if that was convenient for me. Since I just flew two thousand miles out here to try to write this thing, yes, it was certainly convenient for me. But I didn't take it as a good omen that they kept saying that they were confident that we could get "the first treatment down" by the end of the week; that sounded to me as if there was going to be more than just one "treatment," and even though I didn't know exactly what it was, I was pretty sure a "treatment" was certainly not a "screenplay."

Well, it was an interesting start, and this was certainly going to be a learning experience for me, and the food was terrific, so I thought I'd just relax and see what was coming. The veal was outstanding, and they had some sort of pastry thing with ice cream for dessert that may be the best thing I've tasted since Key Lime pie. I nursed my drink through the meal while they had repeats of their cocktails and split a bottle of chardonnay during the meal. They insisted I taste the wine, and it was very, very nice, but like my dad, I'm not much of a drinker, especially when I'm away from home. At the end of dinner, after a lot of "so delighted to be working with you," Doug took me back to the apartment and gave me a card for the car service; they had set up an account in my name, all I had to do was call, and they'd pick me up and take me wherever I wanted to go.

It was nine o'clock, and I was ready for bed … and the phone rang.

"Hello."

"You didn't call, so I thought I'd call you … You okay?" (woman's voice)

"Who is this?"

"Libby ... Libby Shaw ... I checked you in ... I gave you that envelope ...?"

"Oh ... OH, yes ... listen, I'm pretty tired, and it's late, and I want to get to bed."

"Oh, that's right ... you're on mountain time or something ... Yeah, you go to sleep, and I'll pick you up for breakfast tomorrow ... what time's your call?"

"Wait ... wait ... what do you mean?"

"What time do you have to be on the lot?"

"I don't have to be there until two, but I ..."

"Oh, good ... plenty of time ... so how about I pick you up about nine and we'll go eat right here in the neighborhood."

"Wait ... wait ... you don't have to pick me up for breakfast."

"What? Don't you eat breakfast?"

"Yes, I eat breakfast, that's ..."

"Well, great! I'm buying, not to worry ... I just want to talk to you about Rebecca."

"Rebecca ...?"

"Rebecca Boone, Silly ... she's one of your characters ... wait – have you been drinking?"

"NO ... I haven't been drinking ...

"Well I told you I'm perfect for her, and I want to talk to you about it ... Jeeze, don't you remember anything?

"I remember quite well ... it's just that I ..."

"No, no ... that's okay, you're probably tired ... you're from a different time zone and all ... you go ahead and get some sleep, and we'll talk tomorrow ... I'll pick you up about nine ... Nighty-Night."

That was my second encounter with Miss Libby Shaw. I thought I'd better get some sleep and maybe when I woke up tomorrow, I might be back in a world I could cope with a little better.

Apparently not.

The pounding on the door awakened me, and the phone was ringing, and it was closer, so I answered that first: "Hello?"

"Hey … I'm out here pounding on your door … aren't you ready yet? (Her)

"You woke me!"

"Well it's time to get up … you have to be over there at two, and we have a lot to talk about."

"Listen … I don't want to …"

"No, that's all right, you don't have to talk … I know lots of people don't like to talk in the morning until they've had coffee and stuff …"

"It's not just that … I …"

"Listen … If you've got coffee in there, I can fix you a cup while you get dressed, and we could just stay here at your place … if you want?"

"NO … no … I don't want to."

"Okay, then … you get dressed, and I'll wait here in the car … but try not to take too long … okay?" (She hung up)

I sat on the bed for a few minutes trying to figure out what had happened and what I was going to do next. I don't know … maybe I could call the Police and have her carted away; maybe … but then, who knows, she might be able to talk them into locking *me* up; I had no idea what might happen, so I decided to get dressed and go with her and maybe I would find a time when I could escape. This was not how I saw my first day as a "screen writer" going … not at all.

She had an orange Karmann Ghia convertible that must have been from somewhere in the 1970's. It ran, but it was noisy and, it's California, so of course the top was down; between the engine and all the traffic noise a lot of her monologue on the way to Bob's Big Boy was undecipherable. Yes, "Bob's Big Boy," which is supposedly some sort of landmark restaurant where you can still get service in your car on certain days or times of the year or something; I think the servers were called "car hops," or some such thing.

Breakfast was okay; I had bacon and eggs and coffee and she had yogurt and fruit and green tea. It was clear that I did not have to be an active participant in this conversation, all that was required was an occasional nod or an enthusiastic "Yes, yes," and she could apparently go on for hours. She certainly had read the Legacy, and her insight into the character I created around the real Rebecca Bryan was really quite deep and sympathetic; it was not hard to believe that she could understand this character, but, of course, I had no idea of whether she could act or not and no experience in evaluating that craft at all. I did, however, have ample time to just sit back and observe her, and the first thing that was rather astonishing was the color of her eyes: to me they seemed to be lavender. Her pony-tailed hair was long and black as were her lashes and brows, and her skin was almost a light coffee color; maybe not a classic beauty, but something a heck of a lot more than just "pretty." I guessed her age as close to mine, but a few years younger, in her mid-to-late-twenties, with tiny laugh lines around her mouth when she smiled … which was often. She was certainly full of life, and there was something contagious about her enthusiasm which I suspected was likely to make it far too easy for me to just follow along and let her lead me wherever she wanted to go.

When I looked at my watch it was 12:30, and I wanted to get back to the room and brush my teeth and pick up my manuscript and some pens and a notepad. When I told her I had to get back she said, "So, do I get the part?" Well, I tried to explain that I thought she would make a wonderful Rebecca, but I had no idea what the studio had in mind or how any of this casting was done. She insisted that they would do whatever I told them to do if I truly believed she was the only one who could do this role; when I sensed how important this was to her, I thought I should tell her what I really thought about this whole project. I told her what my reservation was from the beginning: that my book was simply a series of short stories, loosely tied together, and I could see no way that it could be turned into a movie. I could see that she was terribly disappointed, but I was unprepared for the transformation. She just looked so helpless, so forlorn, so sad that I could hardly believe it was the same girl; all the fire was gone, all the energy, as if a light inside her had just been switched off. She had some wonderful pipe dream, and I had just made it go up in smoke. I felt awful, and the two tears sliding down her cheeks told me that she clearly felt worse.

There was little conversation as she drove me back to the complex, and I could think of little else to say beyond, "I'm sorry," which only got nods as a response. When I got out, I told her I would call her later and that maybe I was wrong and maybe it would all turn out like she hoped it would; that platitude didn't seem to help much, but she punched her cell number into my phone. She drove away, leaving behind only a small, fragile wave. I felt like shit. So … a perfect warm-up for my first "writer's meeting."

Doug and Clay were waiting for me in a small conference room, which had a sideboard filled with bowls of fruit, platters of small sandwiches, a coffee urn, an electric tea kettle, and a small frig stuffed with water and soft drinks. We sat around this oval table laid out with white ruled tablets and a variety of pens and pencils, and Doug and Clay expressed their concern about my accommodations, my health, my opinion of the weather, my sleeping habits, my adaptability to new surroundings, and a host of other concerns which stopped just short of inquiries into the regularity of my bowel movements. I eventually interrupted the flow by inquiring what sort of schedule they saw for the week. That, apparently was not as easy a question as I thought it was, because the next half hour was devoted to how we needed to "feel our way" through this "process" and not try to set any hard and fast rules, lest we discourage the flow of the "creative juices." Under no circumstances was I to be rushed into any position that I did not fully understand and with which I was not totally comfortable; yes, "TOTALLY."

When we quit for the day, it was just after four. We had not passed one word about writing a script or even a "treatment," and the only decision made was to meet at "two-ish" for the next three days, Friday being "a bit up in the air, schedule-wise" for both of them. Against mild objections, I requested that they each give me a script of theirs to read so that I could get an idea of what a screenplay looked like (and also a peek into their style and content, since we were to be working together.) They grudgingly agreed that they would "try to dig up something" for tomorrow's meeting, and after I declined offers to drop me off wherever I wanted to go, there was a double round of hand-shaking, some mumbling about, "Good start" and the like and my first writer's meeting came to a close.

This had been a strange day, to say the least: I had brought a perfectly lovely, if strange, young lady to tears and then had gone on to learn something about "screen writing," and accomplished absolutely nothing. Really a great start; so, I decided to walk back, get some air and re-think my decision to come out here. I had noticed some tennis courts down the hill from my apartment, and I thought maybe I'd just go over there and sit and watch and forget all about it for a while; I love to watch tennis, and I like to play, although I don't do it much. It turns out this is a nice, small club with a bar and a patio where you can sit comfortably and watch them play, so I bought a beer and had a seat on the patio. There were four pretty good hitters on the near court and about a dozen members drifting in and out, all of whom were having a good time and seemed quite friendly, so I was relaxing when I started to think about Libby. I had promised I would call her later, and since I had ruined her day, maybe I could invite her to dinner and try to do a better job of apologizing. I called.

"Hi."

"Libby?"

"Yeah?"

"It's Buddy McCabe … I was wondering if I could take you out to dinner?"

"Are you *serious*?"

"Yeah … I'm sorry about this morning, and I was hoping I could sort of make it up to you."

"You *are* serious?"

"Yeah … no, no, I'm sorry … this was a really bad idea …"

"No, wait … wait … I think it's sweet."

"Really?"

"Yeah … you were in over your head … and I kinda' ambushed you."

"Well, I don't know … but, yes – I am certainly out of my element."

"Okay, I get off at six … where are you?"

That's how it all started with Miss Libby Shaw.

Tuesday

Tuesday morning was another sunny day, of course. I slept late and decided to walk down to that area where Libby had taken me yesterday and see what other kind of places offered breakfast. Well, there were a lot, and I settled on a diner called Patty's and then walked back to the tennis club to watch some action and have another cup of coffee. It was pretty empty, a mixed double on court one and four ladies on court two; the ladies were all a rank above the mixed foursome. Before long they were all finishing up, and as I was leaving the young man at the desk asked if I was a new member and I confessed that I was an interloper, just a hacker who enjoyed watching the game. He said that there were morning clinics that were open to non-members if I was interested, and that sounded like a heck of a good idea since my involvement in the movie business was probably never going to start before "two-ish." They had a very limited pro shop, but I found a couple of pairs of shorts and shirts that fit and some socks (shoes I have), and Steve, the young man, said that I could rent a racket when I came in for the clinic. I signed up for Wednesday and Friday morning at nine.

The conference room was laid out as before, and my cohorts arrived about ten after with scripts in hand; they had managed to dig something up. We all settled down with coffee and then I asked if they had a starting point in mind for this "treatment," which produced nearly an hour of side-stepping and evasive maneuvers, but eventually boiled down to the fact that they thought we might have to eliminate some of the stories. This was the first thing that made sense to me because I never believed that anybody was actually going to tell ten different stories to a movie audience. They were apparently very concerned that I would be upset by such an idea and that I would not want anyone to tamper with my original material; quite the contrary, I would be delighted to learn how anybody could take my rambling tales and put any part of it on film.

However, I didn't hear anything over the next couple of hours that convinced me that these two guys had any practical ideas about how to do that, unless you call Clay's idea of having Daniel Boone be immortal and become the central character in every story, "practical." Doug's best effort was simply to do the first five and then the last five as a sequel. I started with no idea and ended in the same place, but they were full of confidence that tomorrow would be a different story. We all headed home to think about it.

Dinner last night was on another planet from the breakfast we had that morning. Libby picked this nice quiet Italian place, also in the same neighborhood, and the food was equally as good as the French restaurant. The big difference was Libby: she wouldn't let me apologize and shushed me when I tried; she said it was all her fault, and she didn't want to talk about it. What she did want to talk about was almost all the female characters in Legacy. She wanted to know how I could imagine their thought process and how I could be so sure of their feelings, and she had specific moments that she wanted specific answers for. I had no idea how any of that works, real writers probably did, but I was still just a lucky grocery clerk who found it easy to make up little stories. I really couldn't answer her questions, but she was so savvy and so much fun to listen to and occasionally, when it was my turn, she was an avid listener. It couldn't have been a better evening. When she dropped me off, I got a kiss on the cheek and an invitation for dinner tonight; both of which I humbly accepted.

I walked back to the apartment and started reading Clay's screenplay. It was about a modern family in the mid-west with an over-achieving older daughter and a younger son who was mentally challenged in some way that wasn't clear to me. I had never read a screenplay before and it was slow going; you really have to pay attention to all the directions, which seem to be written in all caps, and not just rely on the dialogue. I was just beginning to understand how writing for film was so concentrated on the visual aspects; this was not a format that I thought I would ever feel comfortable with. When Libby called, about ten after six, I had only gotten about thirty pages into a ninety-page script, and I told her I really had a lot of reading and some hard thinking to do this evening and I didn't think I would be very good company. Well, of course, that was no hurdle for Libby:

"You like chicken, country boy?"

"Yeah, chicken is …"

"You got anything to drink over there?"

"Well, there's coffee and …"

"Never mind. Do you want beer or wine?"

"Oh … a cold beer sounds pretty …"

"I'll bring both, and I'll get us some chicken dinners, and I'll be there in about forty-five minutes … pick up all your dirty clothes and put out some plates and glasses … remember, forty-five minutes."

Thirty-five minutes later, I got a peck on the cheek as my self-appointed caretaker buzzed past me, warmed two chicken dinners in the microwave, popped open a beer for me, and uncorked a bottle of red wine for herself. Soon, we settled down to a nice family dinner. She said she would read one script while I finished the one I was reading and then we'd swap and that way I'd have someone to talk to about my reactions. She told me to go read while she cleaned up; she put stuff in the dishwasher and poured herself another glass of wine and picked up the other script. I hadn't finished my beer.

The next hour was pretty quiet; me in an over-stuffed chair and her curled up on the sofa, reading. Without much chit-chat we traded scripts; she could read scripts a lot faster than I, and the second one, Doug's, was a bit easier for me to get through, about good cops and bad cops in Detroit. Around nine, I put mine down, and Libby had refilled her glass and poured me another beer and was patiently waiting for me to finish reading. I asked her what she thought, but she said, "You first," and I had to admit I didn't think either of them were particularly insightful, but I guessed they were well-told stories. She said, "Crap … cover to cover crap," which I took to mean that she didn't think too highly of them either. I'm not sure exactly what I expected to learn from these readings, but my impression was that it hadn't increased my confidence in this project by one iota. We decided to take a break, and she went to the girl's room, and I stepped out on the little balcony and sipped my beer and began thinking about how far removed I was from this whole world of movie-making. When she came out on the balcony, she put her hand in mine and said, "Don't be depressed … it'll be alright." I didn't know I was depressed until she said so, but she was right; I felt like this was just a big mess and that I had got into something that was never going to come out well. She held herself close to my side and leaned her head on my shoulder; what a wonderful, sensitive thing to do. Then she reached up and kissed me on the cheek and said, "Nighty night … see you tomorrow," … and she was gone.

Wednesday

The tennis clinic was a new experience for me; I had never taken lessons. My pal, Rich, had taught me when I was in high school, and I played once in a great while with someone who came in the store, but I was not a regular tennis player. There were six of us, four older women and a guy about sixty, and the pro was named Ben, and he was very patient, which was a good thing, because I was the second best one there, and I stink. We all chatted a bit after, and I remember a Myra and a Debbie and the guy was Sam, but that was the best I could do, so I hit the showers and walked on over to Patty's for brunch. Then I went to a grocery store and got some eggs, bread, juice, and a melon and a bottle of Merlot for Libby and walked back to the apartment. Then headed down the hill to Warner Bros.

I was a bit nervous that Doug and Clay would ask me about their scripts, but somehow, they didn't, and I was relieved. No one had come up with any improvements on yesterday's session, but Clay suggested that maybe we could each pick the four or five stories that we liked best and concentrate on the ones that appeared on more than one list. Doug suggested that we should really try to find stories that had a common subject or theme, and we also had to start thinking about stories that might be easiest to shoot.

Much to my surprise, perhaps we did have a starting point, or at least *points*: which tales were the best liked, or which tales could be tied together most easily, or the tales that might be the easiest to shoot. It sounded like too many possibilities, but at least they were each a place to start, and we parted with firm commitments to return on Thursday with a list based on at least one of those choices. I felt like my third day in movie-land was already the best so far, and I still had plans for dinner with Libby again tonight.

She picked me up just after six and drove us farther out into "the valley," to a sushi restaurant; I knew what sushi was but never had occasion to try it, so this was another new adventure, courtesy of my lovely tour guide. I let her order, and I couldn't tell you what half of it was, but I really like the seaweed roll things that they cut up into bite size pieces; and Saki is kind of interesting but not destined to be one of my favorites.

She asked about today's meeting, so I went over what Doug and Clay had come up with this afternoon. Even after I assured her that I never believed that anyone could make a movie using all my stories, she was upset that anyone would want to cut any one of them. Sweet, but not productive, so I asked her to come back to my place and help me make at least one list.

As soon as we got back, I put a couple of notepads out on the table and started looking at the titles of all the stories to see if I could find some kind of pattern. This would have been hard if I was doing it on my own, but every time I sort of got a handle on something, Libby was furious that I would leave out this one or that one. I had no idea which ones would be easiest to shoot; Libby said those with the fewest locations, but I shouldn't bother with that, so I tried to find those that could somehow be tied together.

Around midnight, I settled for four stories that simply fell into different generations from 1790 up to 1930; that wasn't much of a connection, but it was the only "list" I could come up with. Libby was decidedly not happy, even though I had started with the one about Rebecca Bryan: "How can you leave out the one about Johanna and her pig? .... about Clementine and the runaway carriage? ... Eva and the piano player?" ... and like that. Definitely not happy! And very argumentative. It was hard to believe how much she liked some of these little stories. But about one-thirty I was exhausted, and so was she. At the door, she gave me a real nice kiss, told me not to worry, and that she'd see me tomorrow. Boy ... I did not want to see her leave!

Thursday

I slept late again and then fixed some melon and scrambled eggs for breakfast and then sat out on the little balcony with my list, to see if it made any sense in the light of day. Just barely. I walked down to the tennis club and watched a foursome of old hackers who were having a hell of a good time poking fun at each other, and for them the quality of the tennis didn't seem to be an issue; I should try to be like that. By then it was about time to get back to the Lot and our two o'clock meeting.

Doug and Clay were waiting this time, so we all grabbed some coffee and sat down to see whether anyone had come up with a list that would show us a path to the "treatment" of this project. Clay had come up with a list based on "easiest to shoot;" all three of those stories took place in or around one character's home. (That never occurred to me.) Doug's list was even a bigger surprise to me because his list contained four stories, all centering on animals. We spent the next three hours trying to decide if any of these lists could really be the starting point. It was strange, but in a way rather nice, that Clay liked mine best, Doug liked Clay's best, and I liked Doug's best. It didn't get us any closer, but it was sure a lively discussion, and about two hours in I decided that these guys were a lot more likely to know what might work than I was, so I just let them argue it out. They finally got around to agreeing that we should try to follow either my "chronological" list or Doug's "central Character" list and keep Clay's "easiest" as a fallback position. It sounded like progress, but when they told me that Morton (Culbertson, the boss) wanted to "take a meeting" with us tomorrow, I was hoping that they would do all the talking, because I was still out in left field, and I couldn't see that we had really accomplished anything.

That evening Libby took us to a place called Chez Nous which was very casual and had a big pastry section. The food was okay, and she ordered a bottle of chardonnay. I had never drunk more than two glasses of wine, so I had no idea how much of that bottle was poured into my glass and how much into hers, so I may have had a bit more than usual.

I told her about the meeting, and she said, "Your list was the only one with Rebecca in it." I realized again how important that was to her, and I felt really bad that I hadn't considered that during our discussions; in fact, I hadn't thought about this from her side at all. I said, "I'm sorry," and she said, "Don't worry, I've been an actress since I was seventeen … I'm used to disappointment." That sounded so sad. I thought what a terrible life that must be, that you just take disappointments for granted. Then we talked some more about my list, but I ended up thinking it was terrible, and I had no idea what I could bring to the meeting with Morton Culbertson.

She drove me back, and I asked her if she'd like to come in, but she said she had to be at work at six tomorrow morning, and besides she saw me yawn once during dinner and I had an important meeting tomorrow. In the car, she kissed me very sweetly before she pushed me away and then, "Nighty night … let me know how it goes tomorrow," and off she went. I was even sorrier to see her go.

Friday

I didn't sleep well, kept waking up and trying to think about what else we could do with my stories; came up with nothing. I fixed breakfast and dropped on down to the tennis club for the clinic. Myra and Debbie and Sam were there and one of the other names I got was Sylvia. Ben worked us pretty hard, and it was fun to get hot and sweaty and forget about all this movie mess. After I showered, I sat around the club and read some of the Tennis magazines for a while and then I walked over to the business area and had a sandwich at a bakery sort of place and ambled over to Warner's to "take" this meeting that I felt totally unprepared for.

Morton Culbertson was nothing if not enthusiastic. He couldn't have been any happier to see me if I was his long-lost brother. He wanted to make sure that "these hacks" had been treating me okay. Doug and Clay laughed on cue. When they told him that we were making selections about which stories to include, he made it abundantly clear that I was to have final approval of whatever they came up with, and he didn't seem at all concerned that, what seemed to me, so little had been accomplished. He assured me that these were "good boys," (although he was maybe five years their senior), and if anyone could find the key to turning my work into a great film, these were the two best on the lot.

His aide, Megan, was about five-eight with acres of blonde hair, an outstanding figure, poured into a low cut, very short lime green dress. She never missed an opportunity to laugh at anything even remotely funny that Culbertson said. Her other contribution to the meeting was continually bending over to fill our iced tea glasses; a sight rather provocative whether facing you or facing away. I never saw her take a note, but I confess I did my best not to look at her too often. Doug and Clay both got kisses on the way out; I settled for a handshake.

Before I knew it, this meeting that I had dreaded was over, and everyone in sight was just brimming with good feelings and confident hopes for the future. Serious handshakes and solid back-slapping, plus many assurances that "We'll keep in touch," put the final exclamation point on my journey into never-never-land. Doug and Clay headed off in one direction and I wandered out through the gate and over to the tennis club to sit and try to do a recap of this strange week.

I got a beer and settled on the patio and sort of half-watched the doubles on court one, but mostly tried to get a little perspective on the last five days. I called home and talked to Mom (Dad was at the store), and I gave her a very brief account of the week's work. She said she'd tell Dad and that I should be careful coming home (I suppose I should mention that to the pilot), and she wanted to check my arrival time … again. That felt good; there was a real world back there, where I had a family and a real job and where, as they say, "everybody knows your name." Then I called Libby and told her I wanted us to go to The Petite Chateau tonight and she said, "Oooh, La La. I've never been there." She picked me up about seven and off we went.

My veal was great, again, and Libby had soup and a huge plate of escargot, and we both had that dessert I liked so much; it's called "profiteroles." I told her about Culbertson and the meeting, and she seemed sure that he was determined to get this picture made and that they would have me back out here in no time. I really wanted to keep in touch with Libby, but I realized then, that I didn't really care that much whether they made the movie or not, and that was kind of a relief.

When we got back to the complex, I asked her to come in and she did, and after we both had a few sips of the wine, I was very comfortable taking her hand and leading her into the bedroom. We kissed and held each other for a few minutes and then we both just got undressed and got into bed like an old married couple. I am still amazed at how natural it all felt. When we finished, she snuggled into my side and put her hand on my chest and patted my heart and said, "I thought we would be pretty good together." I thought it was about a hundred miles above "pretty good," but what do I know?

After a while, she said, "Well, I got to go." That really surprised me, but she said she worked here and lots of people knew her and she didn't want them to see her car here at six o'clock in the morning. I was disappointed, and I asked her if I was going to see her again before I left.

"You're kind of slow aren't you, country boy?"

"I guess …"

"Okay … here's the plan. I'm giving you a key to my place (she did), and here's the address (she wrote it down). Tomorrow, you call your car service and have them take you over the hill, then you can let them go. I'll take us to the ocean, and we can lie in the sun all day and then see how we feel about the night. What do you think?"

I thought I'd snuck into heaven when no one was looking and fallen in love with an angel. She finished dressing and gave me a big noisy kiss on the cheek, said, "Nighty night," and two minutes later I heard her Ghia chugging off into the night ... where was I? ... and what movie?

Saturday

Well, you know how the morning went, because that's where this started. It was about two o'clock when she found a place to park; so, we unloaded the gear and found a spot she liked on the beach. She said it was Seal Beach; it was like a small town with a main street and the like. We picked up a six-pack on the way, and after she got settled, I was assigned to rub the sun-tan lotion on her; not a job I would have given up without a fight. I popped one of the beers and split my time between gazing at the ocean and gazing at her; she was on her tummy with her bra strap opened and her head facing me with her eyes closed. I have to tell you the ocean came in second.

It started cooling off a little after five, so after we found a seafood joint on the main drag, we headed back to her place. I think we both just wanted to be together, so she opened a bottle of chardonnay, and we just sat and talked. We didn't really know that much about each other, except that this felt like something pretty special, so there was a lot of ground to cover.

Like me, she was an only child. Her dad was a studio musician and her mother had been a singer but had barely made a living at it and got a real estate license to survive. She went to Hollywood High, started doing extra work in films when she was seventeen and took acting classes from three or four people I never heard of. I don't watch much TV, but she told me about six or seven shows that she had been on and a bunch of plays she did; I had heard of "The Crucible" but none of the rest of them. She liked her job, because she could always switch hours to go to an audition, or get off for a few days to do a part and it paid well enough for her to get by. I told her all about myself, but we both sort of knew that the thing we didn't want to talk about was what was going to happen next. Libby was the one brave enough to poke the elephant in the room.

"So, what are you going to do, Country? Drag me off to Tennessee, or come on out here and get to work? You can write anywhere, you know."

"I honestly don't know, Libby. I think you would feel as out of place in Brentwood, as I feel here."

"Swell, when you figure it out, let me know … you want to go to bed?"

"More than anything."

"Okay, but don't get all mushy on me, just because this is our last time together."

It *was* different, and I think we both felt kind of awkward about making this time very special. I really didn't like the sound of, "… our last time together." When it was over, she turned her back to me, and I thought she was angry, and she may have been, but she reached back and pulled my arm around her and she held my hand – and we went to sleep, and that's how this extraordinary Saturday ended.

Sunday

We didn't talk much this morning. I couldn't think of anything to say that would solve this problem or make it go away, but I was surprised by her silence; I thought she'd always have something to say. It was a lot like that the first morning when some energy inside seemed to shut off. That Monday morning and that effervescent girl seem so very long ago right now.

She cut some melon, and we had toast and coffee and she had yogurt, which I declined. She was off until six this evening, so she said she'd take me to the airport; my flight was at two-thirty. She took me back to Burbank and waited while I showered and packed, and by then it was time to go. On the way, I asked if we could keep in touch.

"Oh, sure, I'd love to hear more about the grocery business."

"Sorry, I mean … I really want to figure this thing out … I really want to be with you … it's just …"

"Yeah, I know that, Buddy, but what are you going to do?"

"I'm trying to tell you, I don't know … but I want to find a way."

"Yeah … okay."

"Don't be mad, Libby. You know I love you, and I think you love me … but I just don't know how we can be together … it's …"

"Yeah, it's crap … I got that."

"No … I believe it's just a tough puzzle that is probably going to take some time to figure out."

"Well, let me know when you find the key."

A long silence. Then we were at the airport.

While I was getting my bag out of the bonnet and onto the curb, she came around the car and put her arms around my neck and held on real tight.

"I'm just being a shit."

"No, no … it's hard."

"Write me."

"Of course, and we'll figure this out … I promise."

"Don't lie to me, Country."

"Never."

One very long kiss, and I walked away, looking back to see her still standing by her orange convertible, looking very vulnerable … but waving.

I told Mom and Dad all about her, and they both said I should go back out there, if I loved her, and not worry about them, they could handle the store, and if they got tired of it, the Kroger people had made them another offer. I couldn't see them handling the store even with Logan there, and I wasn't convinced that they really wanted to retire. Besides, what would I do out there, and how would I make a living? I started writing a story and got part way into it and then lost interest or I just couldn't figure out how it was going to end, and it had been that way ever since I got back. Libby and I emailed every day, at first, but then she started missing days and lately I only heard from her about once or twice a week; I still wrote every day, but now I didn't really expect a reply, and I missed her more than ever.

Hargrove called once in a while, and asked me if I'd got anything to show him, and the last time, he told me that Warner's said the Legacy was "in turn-around," whatever that meant, but I'd never heard a word from Culbertson or anyone at Warner Bros. We all watched Libby on a TV movie where she played a nun; I thought she was terrific, and Mom and Dad and all the folks in the store that I told to watch thought so too. I figured that her career was going well and all the more reason I couldn't ask her to come out here and give it all up.

I worked a lot and I fished a little, but I couldn't seem to write anything and I was nowhere nearer to getting her out of my mind than I was the first day we parted, thirteen months ago. She was like a shooting star that lit up my life as never before, and then disappeared, never to be seen again.

Last Tuesday I decided to bite the bullet and tell Libby that I couldn't find "the key;" I couldn't figure out how we could ever be together. It was certainly the hardest thing I ever had to write, but I had been brooding about this thing all through the weekend, and I couldn't ask Libby to give up her life, her career, to come live in rural Tennessee, and even if I was willing to try to find some kind of work in California, I couldn't leave Mom and Dad to take care of the store all by themselves. So, I thought, if I told her – if I put it in writing, maybe I could close that chapter and begin to find out how I was going to live the rest of my life … without Libby Shaw.

Thursday, I opened, and about noon, Mom and I were at my desk in the back, sharing the sandwich she brought from home, when I heard a little ruckus up front at the check-out. When I got up there, I came up behind this woman wearing a big hat who was fussing at one of our cashiers, that she "knew Buddy" and she wanted an apron and she wanted to start to work. I said, "Maybe I can help?" and then she turned around, and I saw those lavender eyes. It was her!

"I just flew two thousand miles to see you … don't I at least get a kiss?

"Oh, dear Lord, Yes!" … and she came to me, and I held her like she might fly away. Nothing had ever tasted as good as her lips, not even the profiterole, and I couldn't let go of her for the longest time; until there was a crowd around us and Mom walked up and said, "I bet you're that actress, Libby Shaw … I saw you on television." Well that pretty well got everyone around laughing and broke up our clinch in the best possible way. Mom's good at bringing people back down to earth.

The three of us went in the back, and while Mom called Dad to come over, Libby and I just held hands and stared at each other; Lord, she is *so* pretty! When Mom hung up, Libby started to explain, but she wasn't really talking to me, she was talking to Mom, and she said that meeting her son had pretty much put an end to her ambition for a career, so she expected him to give her a job in the store or figure out some way to take care of her. Mom agreed. Libby told her that all her life she thought she wanted to be an actress, but Tuesday she realized that what she really wanted was to be the wife of a grocery clerk. Mom said she understood completely because almost the same thing happened to her.

Then Libby said, "One other thing, I am absolutely crazy out of my mind about your son." And Mom said, "Me too, but I believe the secret is – not to let him know that."

Well, of course Libby and I got married; that was three years ago. I've never heard from the Hollywood people and Hargrove hasn't called in over a year. Every once in a while, a customer tells me a story about something or someone and I get an idea and, with Libby here, I'm able to crank out another little short story, and I have found a small audience. Well, actually, Libby found me an audience. She put up a sign at the check-out counter inviting anyone to leave their email address, and the next time "famous author Buddy McCabe writes a short story he will send it to you, absolutely FREE." I sent the last one to eighty-seven customers. That's good enough for me.

She also keeps putting up these little signs based on movies, all over the store, like "Gone with The Wine" and "Citizen Kale," and "Streetcar Named Dessert," and like that. Of course, I saved the best news for last: she's pregnant, and it's a girl.

So … I don't know … but it seems to me … she didn't just give me the key to her apartment, she gave me the key to her heart.

THE END

THAT WATSON GIRL

Polly Watson was born on the wrong side of the tracks in a town where most of us were dirt poor and scratching out a living on somebody's farm or in somebody's furniture factory. Her father was mostly a fisherman, sometimes a handyman, and often a drunk. Her mother was a waitress at Dolgren's bar, and her older brother spent most of his adult life in the County jail. Not a lot of role models in her young life and almost all our parents – no, *all* our parents wrote her off as "that Watson girl." What none of the adults seemed to notice was plenty clear to those of us who grew up with her: if she made even a little effort, she was pretty as a picture and as smart as any of us – well, not Zimmerman, of course, but all the rest of us. Polly didn't need anyone's approval except her own. She took guff from no one. I learned later, that included her father. When she was nine, she cracked him on the head with an iron skillet when he pulled her pants down to spank her.

First of all: "pretty;" she had long dark hair, which she usually braided, and it hung down her back all the way to her waist. I asked her what color it was when we were both in sixth grade and she said, "black as night," and that was good enough for me. Her eyes were the kind of blue that sometimes looked like they sparkled, especially when she got excited about something – which was often. And "smart;" not like she was a show-off, but whenever she was called on, she had the answer down pat. Polly got A's or B's in everything. She never had any trouble making friends with the other girls, although she expected a lot from them, so some of them didn't last too long. You had to be careful with the truth around Polly, and you couldn't use bad language. Once we got into high school, she always kept us guys at arm's-length. A fellow could buy her a chocolate soda at Nagel's drug store, or you could take that long walk to carry her books home after school. On rare occasions, she'd go to the movies on a Friday night with one of us. But that was it.

That last one was complicated, because there was no way you were going to get permission from your parents to spend time with "that Watson girl," so you had to say you were with one of your buddies, and you had to be sure he would back you up. Also, you had to leave extra early because Polly would not meet you anywhere; if you were taking her out, you had to call at her front door – end of story. If you thought there was going to be any smooching in the theater, you were way off base; there might be a little hand holding, but only on the way home. If you had behaved yourself, there was this sweet, sweet kiss on your cheek at the end of the evening that made all the fuss and frustration seem like a tiny price to pay. To some of us, Polly was worth it.

Whitesburg is a small town, and ours a small school, so over the course of three or four years of being dating age, we all got to know each other pretty well. Some of the girls were attractive, some not; some were fun to be with, some not so much; some were easy to please, some were almost impossible. Some of the girls were said to go all the way and a few of them, like Polly, were what we called "the untouchables." By the time the Senior Prom came around, most of the guys were trying to figure out which girl was likely to say "yes." I managed to get up enough courage to ask Polly. I was happily surprised when she said yes. Then I just had to explain to my parents why I was taking "that Watson girl" to our most important social event of the year.

I had to listen to a lot of not very nice stuff from my mom and watch a lot of sad head-shaking from my pa, but in the end, they just kind of ran out of things to warn me about and it all quieted down and I even got to use the Olds. I stopped at Craig's Florist and got a corsage and drove out old Simpson Road and, for the first time, pulled up in front of her house in a just-washed four-door car. When I knocked, she asked me to come in; she had always come right out before, so I got a chance to meet her parents and see the inside of her house, which was actually a trailer. It was not very fancy and everything looked pretty old and worn, but clean; her father had on a freshly pressed shirt and it looked like he had just wet his hair down when he came and shook my hand. He was sober, as far as I could tell, almost a head taller than me, kind of mean looking, clean shaven, thin as a rail and just said, "Howdy." Her mother, I had seen at Dolgren's, and she knew me and also shook my hand when she said, "Now y'all have a nice time tonight, but don't stay out too late."

Polly was ... I don't know ... I had never seen anyone look as pretty as she did. She was wearing a black gown that was off her shoulders; her hair was piled on top of her head, and I couldn't stop staring at her. I couldn't even begin to find a place to pin her corsage on, so she had to take it from me and fasten it right above her heart; then she took my hand and led us out to the car. She waited while I opened the car door, and after I got in, she moved across the bench seat to sit *closer* to me … I had trouble starting the car.

The gym looked great, lots of orange, white, and smoky banners to celebrate the University of Tennessee where many of us would be going. Jimmy Bowden's band was playing, and they were really smooth. A lot of us had flasks of bourbon, but Polly didn't want any, so I didn't have any either.

I had slow-danced with Polly a few times at sock-hops, and like most girls she had always put her left hand on my shoulder, but tonight she reached up and cupped her hand around the nape of my neck. I don't know what it was exactly, or how other guys felt about that, or even if girls knew what it did – but it drove me crazy! A lot of guys wanted to dance with her, and each time she would ask me if I minded; I "minded" like hell, but I didn't think I should say that. I kept an eye on them, and not once did she put her hand up on the other guy's neck. We danced every slow-dance like that, and whenever we left the dance-floor she would give my hand a little squeeze before she headed off to the girl's room or wherever. I went outside to cool off – every time.

The last dance of the night was "Dream", and after we took a few steps, Polly put both her arms around my neck and turned her head to snuggle into my chest, and we didn't do much but sway a little from then on to the end. That was nice. That was *really* nice!

Everybody applauded for quite a while after the last tune. Polly squeezed my hand again and went to get her wrap and fix her face or whatever and I stood out front with a bunch of the guys and listened to them brag about how far they got. I just listened. Some of them were going to a party at Marjorie Jenkin's house and some were going to

Chip's Diner up on Highway Eleven and some of them were headed over to park at the Lake to make-out. When Polly came out, I asked her if the Diner was okay, and she said it was fine if we didn't stay too long.

We had some pie, and when I asked her what she'd like to drink, she said she'd like a coke with a little bourbon in it, so we both had a little highball. We didn't stay long, and again she sat *really* close to me on the way to her house. As soon as we parked, she took my arm and put it around her shoulder and pulled my head down and gave me the most wonderful kiss on the mouth I could ever have imagined. I took her in my arms then, and we kissed again and again, and again, until she pushed me away and said, "Let's talk."

"Oh … okay."

"I had a wonderful time with you tonight, Kyle."

"Oh, Polly … so did I. I had a *great* time."

"So, where do you think we should go from here?"

"Uh … what do you mean?

"I mean (and she tucked one leg under her and faced me directly), what happens now?"

"Well … I really want to see you a lot more …"

"Okay, but I mean, do you really want me to be your girlfriend? … and THINK about that before you answer."

"Sure … I mean, I'm thinking about it … and … Yeah! yes, I'd like you to be my girlfriend … it's just I never thought …" I reached over and touched her hand.

"So, what do you think we should do now?

"We could neck some more.

"NO ... not now ..." She took my hand in both of hers and leaned closer to me.

"Listen to me: you're going off to Knoxville in about three months, and there are going to be new people for you to meet and interesting things for you to do ... and I'll be here, working in the library, with no boyfriend and nothing to do but come home from work every day ... so, what am *I* supposed to do?"

"Oh, well, uh ...?"

"If you want to be my boyfriend, you're going to have to start thinking beyond this summer ... and think about what happens to me, when you go away ... okay?"

"Yes ... okay, I will ... I promise."

"All right, you've got a lot of stuff to figure out if you want this to work ... and it's getting late so ... (she uncrossed her leg and leaned back) ... come here and give me a real good-night kiss."

I held her close. She put her arms around my neck. It was a nice, long kiss.

"Now go on home ... I had a wonderful time tonight, Kyle."

So far, that was the best night of my life.

———

That summer was terrific! Polly and I saw each other nearly every day for a soda or a coffee or just a walk from the library back to her house. On a couple of Sundays, we went with some other couples over to the lake. I didn't realize before what a great figure she had – I mean great. She wasn't trying to show off or anything, she just looked ... amazing. Plus, every other Saturday we went to the movies, and the first time I put my arm up on the back of her seat she reached up and pulled my arm down onto her shoulder; I couldn't help wondering, "How the heck does she always know just the right thing to do to make me so darn happy?"

We talked a lot about what the coming year was going to be like, but neither of us had anything like a solution. No busses stopped in our little town; the closest stop was nearly twenty miles down the road, so I had to get a car if Polly and I were going to be able to see each other during the school year. I had some money saved, but nowhere near enough to get even an old clunker that was good enough to make the hundred-mile-a-day trip. I had been working in the shipping room of the furniture factory for the last two summers, but it didn't pay a lot, and I hadn't even thought about saving anything until the beginning of this summer when I got the idea of a car.

After work one day, I walked down to see Mr. Snyder, who runs the Piggly-Wiggly out on Highway Eleven. He had talked to our class once and said there are always jobs coming open in grocery stores and that was a good thing for us to remember. I remembered.

"Mr. Snyder? I'm Kyle Carter. You talked to our class."

"Oh, yeah … I know you … you just graduated, didn't you?"

"Yes. Sir, and I was wondering if I might be able to work for you in the evening or on week-ends?"

"You don't want to work during the day, huh?"

"Well, sir, I work at the furniture factory, Monday through Friday, so…"

"Sounds like you're pretty ambitious, Kyle?"

"Well, sir, I'm trying to save up to buy a car, sir, so …"

"Oh, yeah … every young person has got to have a car nowadays, right?"

"Yes, sir … I guess so."

"What do you do over at the factory?"

"I wrap and pack the furniture, sir – I'm in the shipping department."

"Well … I might be able to find something for you."

"Oh, that would be great, sir!"

"I'll tell you what we're going to do …"

"Yes, sir?"

"We get deliveries every week on Mondays and Thursdays, late afternoon. Now, if you were to come by here after work, I could keep you busy until closing time, getting those deliveries put away properly … what would you think of that?"

"That would be great, Mr. Snyder, that would be great!"

"Well, I know your momma and your poppa, so … I'm going to take a chance on you … and we'll see how it works out."

Thank you, sir … thank you very much, Mr. Snyder!"

"All right, you get in here Monday as soon as you can, and we'll get you started."

"Yes, sir, Mr. Snyder … and thank you again, sir."

That worked out great. Pa drove us both to work every day, and the Piggly-Wiggly was less than a mile from the factory, so I could walk over there on Mondays and Thursdays and then walk home when the store closed at nine. It was six miles, so after I worked that the first night, I put my bike in the back of the car, and I biked home for the rest of the summer. Neither parent was very crazy about this new work schedule because they knew there was going to be a car in my future sooner than they wanted, and that meant "that Watson girl" was still in the picture. Not only was she in the picture, but Polly had her mother get her a part-time job at Dolgren's Bar to help me pay for the car. I really didn't like her working there, for a lot of reasons, but arguing with Polly was a lot like talking to a pretty painting. She was now working Friday and Saturday nights and I was working Monday and Thursdays, so we tried to make the best of the few hours we had together.

I don't know much about it … maybe it's pretty much the same for all young couples when they are first falling in love. It seems that every time I saw Polly, I found something else that was wonderful about her: the way she smelled – shampoo or soap or perfume or whatever it was, it was just like I imagined my girl-friend would smell. The way she put her hand on my cheek each time we met, as she reached up to kiss me; when we were walking, how she would take my arm and squeeze herself up against my side for a few seconds. You see what I mean: Polly and that summer were both terrific!

The first couple of months at UT were kind of rough, for both of us I guess, because I didn't get home until the Thanksgiving break, and when Pa picked me up at the bus stop in Russellville, I had to spend the evening at home, so I didn't see Polly until the next morning. We had been calling each other almost every night, but I was missing her like crazy, and the way she jumped into my arms when I went to the Library that morning, she must have been missing me a little, too. That wasn't the only surprise she had for me; her mother was willing to lend us two hundred dollars so we could get a car! Can you believe it? Between what me and Polly had saved over the summer, we now had nearly five hundred dollars, and we could get a really nice used car for that kind of money.

We spent the weekend car shopping. I got my buddy, Lester, because he knew more about cars than anyone I could think of. He drove us up the highway, as far north as Bulls Gap and as far south as Russellville. He picked out a tan 1960 Ford Fairlane that he said was a steal with only 48,000 miles on it. We took his word for it and bought it on the spot, even though Polly and I both thought it was sort of ugly. We still give most of the credit to Lester for us being able to get through my four years at UT. I came home most every weekend, and Polly gave up her job at Dolgren's, so we were able to see each other regularly that first school year.

That first summer, I knew I could get back on at the factory, but I went to see Mr. Snyder during Spring Break and asked him if he could use me on a steady basis during the summer. When the time came, Mr. Snyder hired me to work full-time in the produce department, and I made more money than I ever did at the factory. Polly seemed okay with her work at the library, but I got the notion that she was getting a little bored. When she said she'd like to work a couple of nights at the Bar again, I felt like I ought to go along with that even though I had a lot of reservations about my girlfriend being around a bunch of drunks. She agreed that she wouldn't work any Saturday nights, which we both knew were the roughest times.

I was lucky enough to make the Freshman team, and it was really the first time in my life that I ever spent any time with black guys. We had played against a lot of high school teams that had some blacks, a couple that were all black, and we generally got along as well as any rival players were expected to, but having teammates is different. I really liked these guys and most of them felt okay about me. Of course, I took a heck of a lot of razing when they found out I came from a place called "Whitesburg;" I had never thought of how my home town must sound to a black person. A couple of these guys were really funny, a lot funnier than any of the guys I went to high school with. Some of it you wouldn't want to repeat around girls, but most of it was just letting the air out of anybody who acted too big for their britches. These guys could really cut you down to size. Tyrene Brown and I became pretty good buddies on and off the court, and we roomed together in our senior year.

Polly and I had started a few conversations on the topic of "marriage," and there wasn't any doubt that we were seriously in love by now, but the practical aspects were a little daunting. I could quit school and probably find work at the Piggly-Wiggly, but we both wanted me to get an education when it was sort of sitting there waiting for me. My parents were still willing to pay for most of that, and in my second year I got a basketball partial scholarship, which became a full scholarship in my senior year. We kind of toughed it out until I got my BS in Business and a Minor in Phys Ed.

Tyrene and I both made the Varsity team in our second year, and when one of the starting guards ripped his ankle, we took turns sliding into that spot. During basketball season, Polly would come up and spend the weekend every once in a while, and I'd drive home most other weekends. That summer, Mr. Snyder moved me from Produce to the Meat and Fish counter, and my last summer he had me order and inventory all Package products, so besides my business degree, I had a pretty good idea of how a grocery store was supposed to function. By that time, Polly and I knew that no matter how impractical it might be, we better do something about getting married, or we were both going to be in *big* trouble. The necking was getting very heavy.

During my last Spring Break, I told my parents I wanted to marry her and went and asked her father for her hand; her father took it a lot better than my parents did, but they could see that this was what was going to happen, no matter what, so they put on a good face and wished us well. We had paid her mother back the money for the car, and we knew that her family was not able to come up with much for the wedding, so Polly and I figured we'd have to settle for whatever the two of us could afford. Mom and Pa said we could have the reception in our backyard and they would take care of the barbeque and the drinks. Pa and I went to reserve the VFW so we could use their huge Seeburg jukebox, which held over eighty songs for a dance on the night of the wedding. I made darn sure they had "Dream" on the list.

I also made a couple of other stops while I was home. I talked to Mr. Snyder, and I was very happy to learn that he had sort of been waiting to see if I would stick with the grocery business. When I told him I certainly was, he said he was counting on having a new Assistant Manager in June. Well, you can imagine how pleased I was to hear that.

My next stop was to see the principal of our high school. I knew that the Track coach had been coaching basketball for the past two seasons, and none of the high school kids thought very much of that situation. Here's what I proposed: "Mr. Spivey, I'll coach your basketball team this season at no charge, and if you and the players are satisfied with me, I'd like you to give me the coaching job next season." Since it was costing him nothing and most everybody in school knew that I had just made starting guard on the Tennessee All-Stars. He thought that was "a Jim-Dandy idea."

Polly's mom and pop found a real nice trailer and paid the first three months' rent on it so it would be waiting for us in June. Polly had mixed feelings about it; she was very pleased with their effort, but we would still be starting our life together on the wrong side of the tracks. I figured, as long as Polly and me were together, there couldn't be anything much wrong with that.

The announcement said: Saturday, the thirtieth of June, ten o'clock at the Baptist Church.

The big day arrived. When Polly walked down the aisle toward me, I thought my heart might explode. We held hands and faced the preacher and ... I married "that Watson girl."

THE END

AFTER KOREA

He walked into my sight, I inhaled, let my breath out slowly, increased the pressure on the trigger and … he fell.

I had pretty good cover, about eighteen or twenty feet up in this leafy tree. I saw the bushes moving about eighty yards away, on the other side of the road. I laid the binoculars down, picked up my scope rifle, and I hit him square in the chest. I had only been up there about twenty minutes so I didn't have any idea if that was the first or last of them. My buddy, Lee, was down at the base of the tree, so he saw the kill and whispered, "Good shot, Luke." I just nodded. I didn't expect my first kill to be that easy.

We decided to wait and see what would happen next before we high-tailed it out of there, because we really hadn't learned much of anything yet. We were scouting the western edge of our flank and were somewhere north of Pyangyong, but we passed that town two days ago and the Lieutenant was the only one with a map, so most of us didn't know diddly about where we really were. Our job was just to see what kind of resistance might be out on the edge of our main force. So far it had been pretty easy going. Casualties hadn't been what you would call heavy, at least in our regiment. Lee and I were both snipers assigned to

Headquarters Company. The whole 2nd Infantry Division was pretty much committed to this move it seemed. We heard MacArthur was running the show, but who knew anything for sure out here?

Me and Lee met in the sniper training camp at Ft Lewis, up in Washington, doing nothing but learning how to improve our shooting skill with the trusty Springfield M1903. I didn't have any idea that I was a pretty fair shot until basic training where they found out I had high scores at long distance targets. Lee and I both went into sniper training right after eight weeks basic. Lee's from Virginia, and I'm from Tennessee, so we sort of know where the other one is coming from, and we get along fine. We alternate who goes up and who stays below on each foray.

Nothing happened for nearly ten minutes. Then I saw movement down the road, and sure enough, another one poked his head out and looked around. I hit him square in the chest, too. Then, almost like it was a shooting gallery at the fair, about ten paces farther down the road another one stepped out, and then another and then one more. I hit each of them in pretty near the same spot. I think they were looking for where the firing was coming from, but not one of them thought to look up. The M1903 magazine only held five rounds, so Lee climbed part way up and we traded rifles.

We stayed another thirty minutes, and by then it was getting dark. It looked like nothing else was going to happen, so I got down, and me and Lee snuck up the road to look at the bodies to see if we could find some kind of identification. They had good warm clothing and gear, and they were all carrying neat looking sidearms and what looked like Chinese rifles. None of them were carrying any pictures or personal information that we could find, but they sure looked like Chinese troops to us. We cut off some epaulets, and two of their caps had marking on them so we took them also, so the intelligence guys could maybe figure out where they came from. We took one of the rifles and one of the sidearms and headed back to base.

After we reported in and told our story to Sergeant Caldwell, he credited me with five confirmed kills and brought us over to the Lieutenant's tent. I got a handshake and a "Job well done, soldier," from him. It was kinda' weird; it didn't feel like I had taken a human life, it was so much like one of the training exercises in sniper camp where you shoot the cardboard targets, – it didn't seem real. When we got over to the mess tent, three or four guys came by and slapped me on the back or hit me on the arm, and I heard "way to go," from a couple of them. I got along pretty well with all my army buddies. I slept okay that night; cold but okay. Korean Winters were pretty cold.

It was late Fall, September 15th, when the Marines hit the beach at Inchon in a surprise attack. By the time our Division landed, the coast and the first five miles or so had been cleared. The harbor was pretty shallow, so we walked across mud flats for the last thirty or forty yards and caught no fire. We re-took Seoul in a matter of days and, like I said, we were well above Pyongyang by the end of October. By mid-November, we were not far from the Yalu River. That's when the trouble started.

I found out much later that MacArthur had sent us up this far against the advice of the Joint Chiefs and President Truman, but that wasn't much help at the time. We were on the west side of the mountains, closest to China, and had just broken camp to start rolling north again when some guys started shouting, "Tanks ... Tanks!" I looked up the road, and sure enough there were three great big Chinese tanks rolling down on us with a bunch of soldiers running behind. I grabbed my rifle, hit the ground and started firing. I'm sure I hit three or four before I got this real bad headache and I must have passed out.

I woke up back in a MASH unit just south of Pyongyang, and they told me it was Thanksgiving Day. I had caught a slug in the left side of my head and a surgeon had removed it about an hour before I woke up. The following week, the whole 2nd Division was trapped in a bottleneck between the mountains, and they were ripped to shreds; Lee never made it out. They tore down the MASH unit and headed south across the thirty-eighth parallel. Six of us on litters were stuffed in the back of a two-ton and driven all the way down to Busan. They only kept me for two days, then I got papers for R & R and shipped out to Japan for an Army camp at Kumamoto.

The Rest part of R & R was okay, but I wasn't up to much active Recreation, so I shot a little pool and went to a couple of Tea Houses in town and saw my first Geisha Girls. Boy, they are something different! I don't remember seeing any Japanese when I was growing up, and I know I never saw anyone dressed like these girls were. They were all bundled up in big kimonos, with something stuck on their back and these big wooden shoes; I sure didn't see anything very sexy about them, but they were nice and friendly, and very polite.

It was around this time that I started getting real bad headaches once in a while, and when I got 'em they pretty well shut me down for a couple of hours; I couldn't focus and had trouble standing up. I also started dreaming about those gooks I killed. Sometimes these guys would get up right after I hit 'em and start walking toward me and sometimes they would just jump up when I went over to check on them and sometimes I would be home and walking down Washington Street and I'd turn around and they would be following me, all of them with big holes in their chests. After that started, even the "Rest" part was not so hot. I went to the medics about the headaches, but they couldn't find anything wrong, so they gave me some pain pills, which didn't do much good. They also sent me to a shrink, and I told him about the dreams, but he said they would probably go away after a while. That wasn't any help either, but I didn't want to make a big fuss about it because I thought they might discharge me with a Section Eight – you know, a psycho.

When you got R & R that usually meant that after you had some time off, you were re-assigned to duty. I expected to rejoin my unit, but I think, since they couldn't do anything about my headaches, they gave me an Honorable Discharge and sent me back stateside. So, even though MacArthur's big surge in November was called "Home for Christmas" and turned into the biggest disaster of the war – I was the only soldier in the entire 2nd Division who got home for Christmas.

Mom and Dad were glad to see me out of the service and that ugly "little war," so Christmas was a pretty good time for all of us. I joined the service in June right out of High School mostly because I didn't really have any idea what I wanted to do. All I knew for sure was I didn't want to go to Med School. Dad was an anesthesiologist over at the Lincoln

Medical Center and I think he wanted me to follow in his footsteps, but that didn't appeal to me at all. Now that I was safe at home, I was still faced with sort of the same problem as before: what was I going to do with myself?

On the ninth of January, I remember it was a Monday. I got a call that was sort of an answer to my question. It was around nine o'clock, and I was in the kitchen having breakfast with Mom. Dad was at work and my sister, Joanne, was in school. Mom answered the phone and then said, "It's for you … someone in Washington, DC." The guy wanted to verify my name, rank, and serial number and wanted to confirm that I was with the 2nd Infantry in Korea. He said he worked for a government agency that was dedicated to helping wounded servicemen find employment. He asked if I would be interested in coming to Washington, taking some tests and seeing what sort of work I might be best qualified for; they would cover all expenses. Well, that sounded pretty good, so I said I'd think about it

I told Mom and Dad about it, and they had no objections, so I called the guy back. He booked me on a Wednesday flight out of Lovell Field in Chattanooga, Dad took the morning off, and he and Mom drove me over to catch a ten-thirty flight to DC. That's how I took the first step toward finding out what I might be doing with the rest of my life.

I had never been to Washington before, but when you fly in, it looks like you're barely missing the tops of the buildings as you land in Arlington.

As I came toward the exit, I saw this fellow holding a sign with my name on it. We went up a sort of parkway and eventually crossed over Key Bridge into what they call Georgetown and pulled up in front of an ordinary looking office building. As soon as I stepped out of the car, this thin little guy came hustling up and extended his hand. "Welcome to Foggy Bottom," he said. I didn't know whether he was being funny or what, but I found out later that's what everybody called this area. Weird, huh?

His name was James McGruder, and he led me inside. We went up one flight and down a long hall, and that's where I met Simon Merkle. Simon was probably in his fifties with greying brown hair, brown eyes, and glasses, just a bit shorter than me, and a bit heavier.

"Can you tell me anything about what I'm doing here?"

"Why don't you take a few of these tests we've prepared, and I can tell you more about it then."

He took me down the hall to a small room with a desk, a folder, and a couple of pencils. He said, "Take your time. I'll be back in a half-hour." It was some kind of IQ test, not unlike what I had taken in the Army, so I finished it and had time to read it over and make two or three changes before Simon got back. He then took me to another office where I met Dr. Gailbreth, a shrink.

Gailbreth wanted to know all about my family and how we all got along and then he moved on to my time in service.

"How did you feel when you shot those soldiers?"

"*Enemy* soldiers."

"Yes, of course – but what did you feel at that moment?"

"At the time, it didn't bother me, but later they kept coming up in my dreams."

"Okay, we'll talk about that in a minute. I want to ask what you see yourself doing for the immediate future?"

"I don't know, really … nothing comes to mind."

"Does that worry you?"

"Not really – I figure I'm young, healthy – I can handle whatever comes up."

"Mmm. So, how do you feel about hypnosis, if we could get rid of those dreams?"

"Sure, let's try it."

He thanked me for my cooperation, said he would see me tomorrow about the hypnosis, and he walked me back to Simon's office.

Simon asked how it went, and I said, "Okay," and he said we should call it a day.

"There are a few tests tomorrow and then we'll know whether we can help you or not."

McGruder came in and walked me out. He said I would be at a Holiday Inn in Arlington, and I could sign for my meals there. Gave me twenty bucks cash for incidentals and told me the Desk clerks could show me where the movie houses and bars were if I wanted to get out.

The Holiday Inn was close to Key Bridge, but I didn't feel like going exploring that night. Seeing D.C. across the river, it sure looked like a beautiful town. I had dinner in the hotel restaurant and then wandered around the business district for a while, had a couple of beers, and headed back to the hotel. I called the folks and told them that I still didn't know much about what was going on, but I was enjoying the experience, and I would probably be home on Friday.

Today started out much like yesterday. Simon took me down to the basement where I got a full physical exam from a Dr. Silverstein. He and his nurse were very polite, very thorough. He examined my bullet wound and asked me if there was still any pain.

"Yeah. Sometimes it's so bad that I can't focus or stand.

"We have something that should help,"

Then he said something to the nurse, wrote me a prescription, and in a minute the nurse gave me a small vial with twelve pills in it. Silverstein said, "One Each Morning. Have it re-filled as long as you need." As I was finishing up, Dr. Gailbreth came in.

We went a couple doors down the hall to a small softly lit room with a couple of over-stuffed chairs and a couch. He asked me to make myself comfortable, so I sat in one of the big chairs, and he sat in the other. He pulled out a little pen-light and held it in front of his chest and asked me to focus on that, take a few deep breaths, relax and just listen. He started talking in a low voice and told me how I was very relaxed and comfortable and that I was even getting a bit sleepy. I guess I was, because the next thing I remember was him saying, "How are you feeling, now, Luke?"

Well, I felt fine … I felt great … very relaxed … like I had just had a nice nap or something, which I guess I did. Then I went back up to Simon's office. He said that he wouldn't be able to tell me any more about the job possibilities just yet because a couple of things had to be cleared up first: the bad dreams and the headaches. I had to admit that there were probably not a lot of people who would hire me if I was going to crap out on them every once in a while.

Simon said there was just one more test he wanted me to take and then they could send me home tonight or tomorrow morning; I told him I'd just as soon leave tonight. We went down to the basement again into this long narrow room with a movie screen at the far end. There was a low counter with a lot of electronic equipment underneath and a rifle. It had the feel of a really light carbine and was hooked up to the electronic stuff below. Simon said he was going to run a film that would be like I was walking through a village and I would come across a lot of different people, some of them regular citizens and some of them soldiers, and I was to try to shoot the dangerous ones and not kill any of the regular people.

He dimmed the lights and started the film. It looked like I was walking down a street, and as I turned a corner, there was a guy aiming a gun at me, so I fired and I could see a red dot on the guy's chest, and a second after I shot him, this little kid poked his head around the corner and I almost shot him, but I didn't. It went on like that for I guess about five minutes; sometimes a woman or a girl or a kid and sometimes a soldier or a guy with a drawn weapon. There was one that was really tricky: this guy in a strange uniform popped out, and I fired at him, but in a split second, I realized he didn't have a weapon, so I jerked the rifle up, and the red dot went over his head. As far as I could tell, I got all the bad guys and didn't kill any civilians. Simon said I had done well, and he'd be in touch.

I spent the first week just relaxing around the house. It became clear that Dad wanted me to be doing *something*, and this wasn't it. I went over to the VFW and talked to a couple of guys and told them I was looking for part-time work. Before the week ended, I got a job over at Bowl-A-Rama setting pins.

After two more weeks I figured that I would probably never hear from the Washington people again. I hadn't had a dream about the gooks since I got home, and I was taking the pills they gave me and didn't have any more headaches, so that part was all good. Three days later, I had just finished setting pins for the Thursday night women's league, had a beer at the bar and was out in the lot heading for my car when this dark sedan pulled up next to me. Simon Merkle leaned out the back window and said, "Luke, I'd like to talk to you."

Well, that really surprised me, him coming all the way down here to see me instead of just calling or something. I got in the car, and he asked me about the dreams and the headaches. When I told him that they were both gone he said he wanted to offer me a job. Simon is Director of the National Clandestine Service, a new branch of the CIA. They are charged with eliminating any problems that the CIA can't handle without compromising their operations. He said, "I think you'll find this job very interesting."

I do. The job is killing moles. Enemy moles.

THE END

DIPPY NOLAN

It all started when Dippy Nolan decided he wanted a new car.

Of course, his name wasn't Dippy, but only his mother ever called him Daniel, and most of his childhood friends called him Danny, but he preferred Dippy, and thought of it as his professional name, which was more or less true because it was bestowed upon him because of how he made his living – even though it was somewhat derogatory. Dippy was a bag man for Alquin "Big Al" O'Leary; he collected the numbers bets placed at various grocery stores, fish markets, barbershops, and newsstands in the neighborhood and brought them to Big Al at the Stag's Head Pub. "Big" Al was not really very large, but Alquin senior was barely five foot five and rather thin; hence his son was "Big" Al. Dippy received his moniker because almost everyone, except Al O'Leary, was pretty sure that he was "dipping" into the receipts before they arrived at their proper destination.

This was true, but Dippy was not as dumb as he looked and, in all fairness, he did look a bit oafish. He was about six-foot-three, and weighed at least sixteen stone (about 225 pounds), and had a huge head with a kind of droopy face plastered on the front of it. His size surely had something to do with Big Al's confidence in him to safely transport the cash through the neighborhood, but O'Leary admitted that he had a kind of a soft spot in his heart for Dippy because he reminded him of a hound he had when he was a kid. At any rate, Dippy was savvy enough to take only a Euro or two on slow days and only slightly more on regular days, and he waited patiently for those "hot" days when his pockets were so full that they affected his gait; then he loaded up. So far, he'd never been caught. Or, maybe Big Al figured it was just part of doing business.

Now he wanted a new car. He got his first car from Slick, over at Murphy's Garage four years ago, and it wasn't new then, and now he wanted something nicer – something shinier. The way it worked was, if you saw a car that you liked, you described it to them, and then in a few weeks, they would find one for you, and if you liked it, you settled on a price. Dippy didn't know how or where they got their cars and figured it was none of his business anyway because they were always willing to negotiate the price and that was all that mattered to him. Well, he saw this Audi that was dark blue and looked neat to him, so he thought he'd go talk to them. The older one was Murph, and the younger one was Slick, and like Dippy, Slick had a juvey record, and he felt they could talk straight with each other.

Three weeks later, Dippy was driving a bright, shiny, dark blue Audi that Slick said was less than two years old … and I wandered into the middle of it.

I don't believe there are any slow periods in the criminal world; a time when the crime rate drops. There are far too many people, all over this vast globe, who will not play by the rules, who want what's not theirs, who take the law into their own hands, who lie and steal and cheat and kill as if the rest of us don't matter at all. That has always made me angry, and that is probably why I do what I do. But I hadn't had a posting in more than three weeks; my younger sister, Bridget, just emailed me that she was about to deliver her fourth child, and it was my older sister, Mary Alice's birthday next week. The clincher was, I had more than a week's vacation time about to expire. It seemed like a good time to go home and reconnect with my family for a while. I hadn't been back since Mamma died, nearly five years ago, and if Interpol really needed me, they could always find me.

It's more than four hours, closer to five, to fly from Lyon to Dublin, so I decided to take the train to Paris, about an hour-and-a-half, and get a non-stop to Dublin, which is less than two hours. The time worked out to be about the same, and so did the Euros, but my way let me relax in the club car on the way to Paris, and not be all cramped up in one of those ever-smaller airline seats in Coach, because this was my money and I wasn't going to be sitting in Business Class on the Interpol expense sheet this trip. At the time, I was a little over halfway through my second read of *Portrait of The Artist as a Young Man*, so the train trip allowed Mr. Joyce and me to get together again for about an hour-and-a-half. Joyce makes me crazy, but I love him.

On the Flight to Dublin, I opened him again, and he got me started thinking about my own family. My da' died when I was sixteen, and Mary Alice, who was twenty then, became our "other" mother, and although she was plenty hard on us, she always understood the problems we had and the troubles we got into a little quicker than Momma, and it seems to me that we still look to her whenever there's any kind of a problem. Bridget is the beauty in the family, long tresses of auburn hair with highlights of Mamma's red in it, and lighter blue eyes than any of the rest of us. She never had to ask anyone for anything, twice. She married a bank clerk, Edmund Malone, who is also a Deacon at St. Peter's, right after she graduated, and to help out, she sews for a few friends and neighbors. Although they're not wealthy by any means, they seem very happy and pleased that their fourth child is on the way. Mary Alice has only one girl, Theresa; she's an eight-year-old, raven-haired, dark-eyed cutie, with proper manners and shy as a colt. Mary Alice married a stone mason, Devin – just like her da' only not a drunk – and she teaches sixth grade at Mt. Carmel across town.

And then there's the other one – my kid brother. I try not to think of him because he makes me so mad; mad at him, mad at me because I couldn't help him, mad at all those sods that he ran with, who led him away from us and turned him into little more than a crook. In three years, he migrated from a dependable altar boy to a rebellious teenager to a delinquent with a juvenile record and the nickname, Slick. Nothing any of us said to him could get him straightened out; he was hell-bent on going his own way, and to my way of thinking that was all downhill.

Mary Alice and Devin have a guest room, so I drove my rental to their place in our old neighborhood and swallowed a big shot of nostalgia as soon as my foot hit the sidewalk. Henrietta Street has changed a great deal for the better over the last forty years, and they have a very neat and roomy, second-floor apartment that looks like a mansion compared to our old tenement over on Gardiner Street. When we were kids, we lived in the slums – we just didn't know it at the time. Now, most of those old neighborhoods like Gardiner and the Sheriff Street flats have either been demolished or seriously gentrified.

Devin, like many guys who work with their hands, is an uncomplicated soul, and since it's clear as the stars above that Mary Alice loves him, he's always been very easy for me to get along with. He also went to the trouble to lay in a fifth of Jameson's for my stay – clearly a Prince among men. After dinner, Devin asked if I wanted to go out, or watch TV or what, and I realized what I really wanted to do was to sit in a real home, with some people I loved and do nothing. He put on a record of some old Irish folk songs, poured us a dram of Jameson's, and we both hummed along with a few of the tunes we knew. After a while, Mary Alice and Theresa joined us. Theresa was in her pajamas and crawled up in her mother's lap, and Mary Alice started telling her "The Piper's Tale," just as Mamma had told all of us. I sipped my drink, leaned back in my chair, and drank in the sweet, sweet sound of my native tongue as it was meant to be spoken. It washed over me, as refreshing as a cool April shower, and I thought to myself, "Oh, my Ireland … 'tis true – there is no place like home."

SEAN

Ever fool knows you don't pull no fruit off your next-door neighbor's tree, so when I start shopping for a vehicle, I cross the Liffey and head south for a couple of miles before I even start looking. I generally go after work, and I start down about Herbert Park and start working the big parking lots going west as far as Harold's Cross Road and then start coming back. Dippy come by on a Saturday, so I didn't feel like starting until Monday evening, and it wasn't until Friday night that I come north over the Grand Canal and eased over toward Griffin College, thinking "college kids? sure and the rich ones could be driving an Audi," and there it was: a nice silver A4 sitting on the end of a row.

I pushed the "slider" down the driver's window, jiggled a time or two, and she was open; I put her in neutral and hooked up the tow cable, and I was out of there in less than five minutes. Easy as pie. First thing I did, I filed off the VIN and removed the spec plates on the driver's door and put a good coat of boot black on all four tires. To do a really good paint job, you got to do a lot of hand work on the door frames, the engine carriage, and the trunk; you can't just sandblast it and spray it in the paint room and forget about all those little hidden spots. That takes time, and I like to spend time with these babies. It's amazing how you can change their looks, I mean like a plastic surgeon or something. I spray painted the rubber floor mats, steam cleaned the engine, and pulled down a set of really expensive looking seat covers and then hit the whole insides with a canister of that "New Car" stuff we got. It was looking cherry and smelled practically brand new; then I set the odometer back to just over nineteen thousand kilometers and figured, "Yeah – less than two years old." Hell, her owner would never know her.

———————————

Next day, I took Bridget to lunch at the Winding Stairs Bar, down on the Quay; there's a bookstore on the ground level, and upstairs, a decent eatery, just as I remembered. She certainly looked to be on the verge of delivering, but that face could still stop traffic, and she got a serious amount of attention at the restaurant. She filled me in on all the wondrous doings of the three left at home with the babysitter and assured me that she and Deacon Edmund were getting along just fine.

But she urged me to go see brother Sean, just as Mary Alice had yesterday. I said I'd think about it; I put her in a cab, and after I'd picked up a book for Mary Alice's birthday the next day, I walked along the Liffey up to the Old Abbey Theatre, just to look around the lobby and see what was playing.

When I got back to Mary Alice's, she had gone out to some sort of class that she needed in order to maintain her teacher certification, so Devin and I ate at his neighborhood spot, Carl's Pub, which seemed to me to be a name totally lacking in both imagination and historical significance. However, the Guinness pipes seemed to be well tended, so I had no complaints.

About ten o'clock he got a call from Mary Alice; her car had been stolen. There are no shortcuts through the center of Dublin and it took us over a half hour to get down to where Mary Alice had been taking her class. She was crying and beside herself, partially with guilt and partially anger; I assured her it was in no way her fault – car thieves can get into any car if they really want to, and I went to find the copper in charge of the scene. He was not too impressed with my Interpol credentials, but when I told him that I used to be a sergeant in the Garda, he saw me as one of his own. Although I pressed him, he really had no leads and nothing to go on. This kind of crime is too casual and happens far too often for any copper to be expected to spend a lot of time on it; in Dublin, he said, "thirty to forty a night." He did go back to Mary Alice to make sure he had all the details she could give him about the car and the time frame, but neither of us had much hope of finding this car until the thief or thieves were through with it, and the most likely story was, it was already being chopped up for parts.

When we got home, Devin paid the babysitter and then fixed us a spot to drink, and we sat around talking about how frustrating these things are. Devin reported it to their insurance company and kept telling Mary Alice not to worry, that they would get this all straightened out in a day or two. I like the way this guy takes care of my sister, and I was feeling pretty useless myself; then it occurred to me that our kid brother worked for Uncle Jamey who had a car repair shop, and maybe one of them might be able to come up with some kind of information about "chop shops." I told them that I would get on it first thing the next morning.

At nine a.m., I called Garda Headquarters and asked for Officer Jim Hennessey, a guy I was a cadet with twenty or so years ago. I was informed that it was "Inspector" Hennessey and I was connected to another officer whom I asked if Sergeant Michael Murphy could speak with the Inspector: and a second or two later, I heard that familiar brogue asking, "It's really you, Mike?"

"It's me, Pig, how you doing?"

"Pig" got his nickname from our two years at the academy because he could seemingly eat his own weight in food at every meal and never show it. We traded catch-up stories for a couple of minutes and then I told him that my sister's car was stolen last night and wondered if he could think of anything to do. He said he'd call Tommy Thomason, another cadet pal of ours, who was in Burglary and Theft and have him get the word out that a "cop's car" had been stolen. He took all the particulars and wanted me to come out and have lunch with him and Tommy, but Headquarters was all hell and gone out in Phoenix Park, so

I begged off for today but promised we'd get together before I went back to the continent. Then I drove over to Uncle Jamey's garage on Mayor Street near the docks to see if he and my kid brother could point me toward any "chop shops."

Uncle Jamey is Da's youngest brother, the last of the four boys alive, and a man I remember as always being a bit grim; even at the gayest of wakes he never seemed able to join in like his older brothers, and I never felt very close to him. Sean and I had been wary of each other since he was a teenager, so I didn't expect a lot of cooperation from either of them, but it was the only place I could think of to start doing *something*.

Garages are, by nature, rather grubby places, but it felt like this one took special pride in being as greasy, and dank and smelly as possible. Neither Uncle Jamey nor Sean could think of another mechanic, who was into any such "nefarious business" as chopping up stolen cars. Both were lying through their teeth, even though I had told them that it was Mary Alice's car that I was trying to trace. But before I even got around to describing the car, at the mention that it had been heisted from Griffin College, Sean started a coughing fit and looked like he had just swallowed a week-old piece of fish. He went off, hacking away, and since Uncle Jamey didn't seem to have anything else to offer, I gave it up.

Today was Mary Alice's birthday, and Bridget's husband had made reservations for all nine of us at his friend Timmy Keogh's Café down on Trinity Street. Devin and Mary Alice and Theresa and I took my rental down across the Liffey, right near the Bank of Ireland where Edmund worked, and I got to see Bridget's three beauties for the first time in five years: Colleen, Erin, and Siohban. They were all blessed with their Mother's grand looks, and their grandmother's red hair, and they were so well-mannered that I felt I had to "watch me P's and Q's," so as not to embarrass them. Terrific little ladies, but I got the feeling that Edmund Malone wouldn't mind if the fourth child was a boy. We had a bountiful meal, a huge helping of laughter. Mary Alice forgot about her missing car for a while, and I had an evening with my family that I would cherish for many a year to come.

SEAN

When Mike said "Griffin College," me heart come up in me throat and I thought I would cough me head off. When Uncle Jamey asked me what was wrong, I just laughed it off 'cause he don't know where the car come from, all he knows is that we colored it. But – Jesus, Mary, and Joseph! … it can't be that I boosted me own sister's car; no … no … that's *too* much! And now I've got a brother who already hates me, hot on my tail, and he's a copper, and when he finds out that it's *her* car, he'll kill me for sure! What am I gonna' do … what am I gonna' do?

Calm yourself, boyo, calm yourself … let's just take a breath here and let's see if we can look at this little problem as a "car" problem and not a "family" problem; 'cause I can "fix" cars.

All right … all right, here's what I can do – I'll go to Dippy and explain that the former owner … no … no, that's no good; Dippy don't care, and he would slap me up the side of the head with one of them ham-hock hands of his, and that would be the end of it. Okay, then … okay … what I've got to do is find *another* Audi, never mind the color or the model, I can color that, and get it to look enough like Mary Alice's to fool her, and … Yeah, that's more like it! I like that!

Okay, then … I got to get on this; I got to find me an Audi before the night is over and get it back here and get it colored before the copper comes snooping 'round again, or figures this thing out. Me brother is a bloody bulldog once he gets onto something. So … let's get on it.

The bedside clock read three-thirty in the a.m. when my mobile rang and I heard Tommy Thomason say, "Michael, it's Tommy, we've got a bit of a problem here and I think you better come on down to the Fitzgibbon Street Station. It's about that car." I was dressed and standing at the Front Desk in about twenty minutes. Tommy came out, he looked as trim as ever but with some grey along the sides, and took me back to the Booking Room, and told me to sit; I did, and he told me the story.

The Garda had picked up Sean in a used car lot on Dorset Street, hooking up an Audi to his tow-truck at two-twenty this morning. They called Tommy because The Daily Bulletin said he was to be contacted immediately regarding any new information on stolen Audis because they might be a cop's car; when he got here and found out it was Sean, he called me. Sean was in a holding cell but no charges had yet been written up. Tommy took me back and left us alone.

"Mike, I'm sorry … I'm really sorry … I know you don't need all this."

"Let's not worry about me, right now; why don't you tell me what's going on with you, Little Brother." And he did.

Of course, he couldn't know it was Mary Alice's car he boosted, but when he found out, he was trying to get another one for her to replace it, and that's why he was in a hurry and got careless and they nabbed him.

He confessed he had started doing this four years ago, on Uncle Jamey's suggestion, and by now he believed it was expected of him as just a matter of doing business. When he finished, he was still saying, "I'm so sorry," and he was almost crying, and I was mad enough to kill. Why didn't our bloody uncle try to straighten him out instead of leading him in the wrong direction? I knew some of this was Sean's fault, but as I saw it, he was a simple lad who had wandered off the path and was taken in by a "Fagin" of the lowest order, and encouraged to steal, and … he was my brother. I asked the Guard to get him some hot tea, and I went to talk to Tommy.

I'm a lucky guy, and I know it, and maybe this whole side of the Murphy clan is lucky as well, because when I read the report it stated that the car had not actually been *moved* when they grabbed Sean. I pointed this little detail out to Tommy, and he grinned and said they "couldn't hold him on such *flimsy* evidence," and signed him out. I asked Tommy if there was anything I could do for him, and he said, "Show up for lunch with me and Pig." I told him it was a done deal, collected Sean, and we went off to breakfast.

SEAN

When he got me out of the slammer, he asked me where we could get some real hash browns, so I told him the Golden Cock over on Eccles Street, and we settled into a booth in the back. We downed the food without much conversation, but then we went through two pots of tea and did more talking than I guess we ever done in our life all together. We're brothers; you don't *talk* to your brother; you scrap and argue and hit and shove and mostly just wish they'd leave you the hell alone. But somehow, since he'd gone away, me brother, Mike, had become not only a talker but a guy who could get me to talk, and I did.

Around eight, he said he had to make a couple of calls and stepped outside; we'd been sitting here for near on two hours. He was gone about twenty minutes. When he come back, he said, "Let's go," and he took me back to me flat on Railway Street and told me to pack me gear. Well I said, "Now wait a minute here," and he put a hand on both me shoulders, and put his face right up to mine, and he said, "You're leaving this neighborhood, and you're leaving Uncle Jamey, forever, and I want no back talk on the subject." From the look in his eye, this didn't seem like a good time to discuss it, so I done what he said. Then he took me over to Fatima's House on Gardiner Street, a real nice B & B, and paid them for two weeks; he said, "Until you get settled," and I dropped my stuff, and we took off for the car lot on Dorsett Street where I had tried to boost that Audi.

This really seemed like a bad idea to me because I might not be too popular there, but he said none of the people working there could possibly have seen me or have even heard my name, and if I liked the looks of the car as a replacement for Mary Alice's, then "maybe we should get it for her." I didn't know how in hell I was going to pay for half a car, but Mike said we'd work it out, and I sure liked the idea of trying to make it up to me sister for what I done. The one I was going to boost was a year younger than Mary Alice's, which was way to the good, with a lot less mileage, and it was the right color, and it was an A4. Mike asked what I thought of it, so I fired it up, looked it over good, crawled under, and told him it was cherry, and he went in and spent about a half hour talking to the salesman and a couple other guys, and when he come out, he said, "Okay, now let's go see Mary Alice."

Jesus, Mary, and Joseph! … I told him that was a stinking' idea, but he told me it had to be done; then he said, "Most times, it's best to do the hardest things first." I thought about that a lot of times after he went back to France, and I finally come to thinking, maybe there was something to it, but right then, I was sure he was full of shite. He didn't seem to have a care about my opinion in the matter, so off I went to face me oldest sister and explain to her why her dumb-ass brother had heisted her car. Yeah, this was going to be one of me favorite days ever.

———

Yesterday, Mary Alice sat like a stone while Sean stumbled through his confession about her car; then she got up, crossed the room, pulled him to his feet, and held him in her arms, with the tears streaming down her face. He was not to live in some "boarding house." He was to live with them until "things got straightened out." Devin had no objections, and Sean and I knew better, from long ago, than to argue with her. So as soon as I headed back to Lyon, Sean was going to be moving into their guest room.

I asked Devin to take them to the car lot so Mary Alice could pick up her "new" car. I had huffed and puffed a lot at the dealers and flashed all kinds of foreign badges, and sort of shamed them into accepting my check for a thousand Euros so my poor sister could have a car to drive. We didn't dwell on why she didn't have one, but finally they agreed to my handling the rest of it on a monthly plan, and Mary Alice could come sign for it and drive it away. Meanwhile, I was off to meet Pig and Tommy for lunch at the Copper Penny out near Garda Headquarters.

I'm sure it's just one of those "guy things," but when the three of us started talking about, "back in the day" when we were all cadets or dumb ass "beat cops," I swear the air was blue with the coarsest profanity ever heard. Those were good times then, and these are good times now, and the three of us knew that in our profession it was only by the Grace of God that we were alive some twenty years later. These were good men, and while I was with them, I was pleasantly reminded that I came from that corps of good men who had sworn to "protect and serve."

I just barely brought up the subject of finding a job for Sean before Tommy jumped in to tell me he had a buddy who "owed him one," and there would be a job waiting for an experienced mechanic in the Garda Motor Pool Garage whenever my brother gave him a call. We all drank just a bit more than needed, Pig still ate twice as much as either of us, and "lunch" didn't break up until after three. We all swore it wouldn't be a decade before we bent an elbow together again; not sure that any of us believed it. I drove home rather on the careful side, and Mary Alice sat us all down to a wonderful stew that evening, and after she put Theresa down, the four of us sat around gabbing until well after midnight, and then I drove Sean back to the B and B, and hit the sack.

———

At four o'clock this morning, Mary Alice shook me awake and said, "Bridget just had her boy – let's go see him." I had a sort of a long and busy day yesterday, and I thought they would both still be in hospital at eight or nine this morning and I could go see them then, but Mary Alice was of a different mind, and that was the end of it. Devlin, Theresa, and I piled into Mary Alice's "new" Audi and headed out to Bon Secours Hospital up off Route 108; Mary Alice proudly driving.

Bridget was radiant; Edmund looked as if he was a foot taller than yesterday, and of course, all new babies are beautiful; this one could have been ugly as sin and he would still have broken my heart into the same number of pieces. When Edmund and Bridget said they had decided to name him after me, I thought it was the proudest moment of my life, and when she let me hold him, I knew it was.

Sean arrived (Mary Alice had called him, of course), and there was more hugging and laughing and congratulating and "ooooing", and after about a half-hour the nurse shooed us all out and got Bridget ready to feed her "Michael" for the first time. We went down to the cafeteria for some breakfast, and I started to make arrangements for my return to Lyon; today was Sunday, and I was due at my desk Monday morning. There's no non-stop service to Lyon, so I had to settle for the five-hour return trip with the hour layover in Paris. I was headed "home," but I had never felt like Dublin was my "home" any more than I did right now. This had been some kind of week, and the last couple of days were the toppers.

I'd regained a lost brother, re-experienced the overwhelming love of my oldest sister, had a nephew named for me, and bonded with two true buddies from my youth. A bit more than I bargained for when I decided to take a week off from crime, but of course, I hadn't escaped "crime" all together, and if Dippy Nolan hadn't wanted a new car, and my brother hadn't boosted it, who knows whether any of this would have happened.

Maybe I should send Dippy a fifth of the good stuff.

218

THE END

THE PRINCESS, THE FROG AND THE FOOL

THE PRINCESS

Long ago and far away, in a verdant valley way beyond the mountains, lived a beautiful young Princess named Miriam, with her parents, the King and Queen of this tiny Kingdom. As the Princess grew up, she was taught to care for all her subjects, and that with the power of royalty comes great responsibility. She was taught to curtsey, how to address other royalty, how to dance, and how to receive her subjects gracefully.

She was not only a lovely child, and a bright one, but also a most obedient one – and grew into adulthood beloved and admired by all who met her. As a young Princess, she was much sought after, not only for her royal position but also for her beauty and generosity of spirit. For this young woman dedicated many hours of almost every day to feeding and caring for her subjects. She worked long hours in the dining hall making sure that the cooks and servants provided all the peasants who came with proper food and drink. Thus, there were many in the kingdom who loved Princess Miriam.

Busy as she was in her own kingdom, this adventurous young beauty was constantly seeking out other realms to visit, and was welcomed and admired in regions near and far. As knowledge of her beauty and charm spread, royal and powerful suitors arrived from many parts of the globe to seek her favor. So, it came to pass that there were many balls and festivals and outings that the Princess had to attend and, because she was so courteous and considerate of everyone's feelings, she was often entertaining the visiting royalty until the wee hours of the morning. But she never complained because she seemed to like almost everyone she met and found it quite easy to become their friend. And her life was very full.

One day, she was walking a different path in the forest surrounding the castle, when she came upon a clearing where an elderly man invited her to join him for a simple meal of fruit and nuts. He was very courteous and had a curious twinkle in his eyes that made her feel quite comfortable, so she agreed. They sat together on the banks of a small pond in the clearing and began to talk. He knew at once that she was a Princess, and she learned that he had spent his whole life as a court jester in a land very, very far away. When his King became old, he had given his jester a bag of gold coins and told him to go wherever he pleased. Wanting to see more of the world, he had wandered to this peaceful glen and cared for whatever denizens needed his aid, for he had a great rapport with almost all animals. Cats – not so much. They talked, easily, for over an hour – she telling him of her work in the dining halls, and he telling her stories of days long gone, and another Palace and another Princess. Since she had enjoyed his company and his wry humor, she promised to return and have a meal with him again.

The Princess continued her generous work in the dining hall, still attending a number of late-night balls, and still travelling to visit distant friends, but she also began to look forward to her quiet meals with the elderly jester. On a later visit, she detected something in the old man's eyes that spoke to her of a tenderness like she had never felt before, and before she left that afternoon, she realized that she was quite fond of this quaint old man.

On her subsequent visits, they talked more freely than ever before – she allowing him to share some of her more private thoughts – and he, juggling for her and disclosing some of the tricks of his trade. She felt herself growing much closer to him. On this particular day, she had talked to him of deeply secret things that she had never before expressed aloud, and in so doing she felt a lightness in her heart – a freedom – as if a weight had been removed. His attention to her made it easy to talk to him, and his responses were so comforting and understanding that she was moved to tears. After they finished their simple meal by the pond, and he was walking with her to the edge of the clearing, Princess Miriam, overcome with gratitude – turned and kissed him.

What happened next, dear reader, is part of a quite unusual story, which began in a land even farther away.

THE FROG

In this land even farther away, and many years ago, lived a lovely Princess named LeeAnne, whose parents doted on their only child and tried to fulfill her every wish. She was quite lovely, and renowned for her pristine complexion and alabaster skin. When she awoke one morning – with of all things – a wart on her hand, you can imagine that there was great consternation throughout the Palace. All manner of potions and remedies were suggested by Councilors, hand-maidens, learned scholars, fishermen, visiting clergy, minstrels, village crones and, of course, the Royal Alchemist. Many were tried – but with no success – the young Princess was desolate, and her parents were furious that nothing could be found to help their beautiful child.

This terrible state of affairs had continued for several days when the Queen was informed that one of the scullery maids had been similarly affected and had since been cured. The maid was summoned, at once, and with great trepidation and much hesitation she began to explain what she had done to rid herself of this plague.

Tentatively, the scullery maid began: "My gramma said that everyone knows that playing with frogs can get you a wart but …"

"Go on, girl. What about getting rid of them," the Queen scolded.

"Yes'm," the maid continued, "Gramma said that you can also get warts to go away if you can find a frog and …"

"And, what, girl? – speak up," the Queen nearly yelled at her.

"Well, your Majesty – she said if you kiss the frog, the wart will disappear," the terrified maid said.

You can imagine that there was quite a furor among the members of the Court and the Royal Family, about the propriety of their Princess "kissing a frog." While the Princes said that she was willing to try anything to rid herself of this monstrous blemish, and some members encouraged her, the King and Queen and the majority of the Court had grave doubts about the efficacy of this tactic and felt it was quite improper for a Princess to deport herself in such a manner. Since it seemed that this debate was going to continue for many hours, the

Princess decided to slip away with one of her handmaidens and try this strange remedy without anyone knowing.

It so happened, in this land so far away, that on a lovely lily pad, in a lovely pond in the middle of the lovely Palace garden, lived a splendid frog. He was not a particularly handsome frog, but pleasant enough, in excellent physical shape, a superior jumper, with a keen mind and a remarkable ability to communicate with other animals. Most of whom referred to him as "Fred." He was well liked and respected, not only by other frogs, but by many four-legged creatures who dwelt on the Palace grounds. It was not unusual for a dog or raccoon or a fox to seek his advice on matters of protocol and courtesy. Cats – not so much.

On this certain Sunday afternoon, he was sunning himself on one of the larger lily pads, while chatting with two young frogs about the far-reaching effects of climate change, when Princess LeeAnne and her handmaiden appeared at the edge of the pond. Upon seeing the Princess, he immediately shushed his comrades, bowed gracefully and sat erect, waiting to see Her Grace's reason for visiting his domain. The Princess, who had never before visited this pond or this frog, commanded her handmaiden, Esther, to go into the pond and fetch her a frog. Of course, as soon as Esther hiked up her skirts and stepped into the pond, both of the young frogs hopped into the tall grass surrounding the pond and disappeared from sight. Sensing the Princess' intention, Fred (for that is what we shall now call him) hopped gracefully over a series of lily pads and alighted on a small tree stump just next to her.

The Princess was taken aback and quite unable to figure out why the frog came to her or what she should do now that he had. Touching him seemed a lot ickier than she had previously thought – if, indeed, she had actually thought of that aspect of the "remedy" at all. She called to Esther to get out of the pond and help her figure out what they could do, now that this opportunity – meaning Fred – had clearly presented itself.

Although, she decidedly did not want to go through life with this ugly wart on her hand – she complained to Esther – the prospect of actually having to kiss a frog may be more distasteful than she could handle. Esther had no solution at the ready, so the two young ladies sat on the lovely grass by the side of the lovely pond, and pondered the frog sitting quietly on the lovely tree stump before them.

Having overheard the Princess' complaint, Fred, 'though slightly dismayed that she should find him unattractive, realized that he might have to encourage her, if he was to be of service to the daughter of his King. So, to get the ball rolling, so to speak, Fred said, "Please kiss me," and closed his eyes in anticipation. What the two young ladies heard was probably something like, "Gleet gig glee," but, whatever they heard, the Princess was still no closer to kissing a frog than before, and just as much in the same dilemma. When Fred opened his eyes, he realized that the Princess was apparently unable to make this tiny romantic gesture on her own and, as is often the case, he – as the male in the relationship – must take the initiative. So, without any thought to his own safety, Fred leaped across the space separating them and kissed the Princess soundly on the lips.

Well – you may have heard actresses in horror films scream, but you have never heard a scream like the one LeeAnne cut loose. Esther lost her hearing for more than a week. Two Royal glass vases in the throne room were shattered – and that was over 400 meters away. Thirteen koi were tossed up onto dry land by the tsunami created in the pond. And two crows dropped dead from fright. This was a serious scream. The Princess then bolted to the Palace to wash her face – and especially her lips – for the next forty-five minutes.

The wart disappeared in a matter of hours, and the entire Palace was in a celebratory mode for days on end. The Princess LeeAnne was lauded for her bravery and audacity, and even her parents had to admit that she took the most practical course. But, back at the pond, an even stranger story had begun to unfold.

THE FOOL

It was no small surprise for the frog to find himself nearly six feet above the ground. Even during jumping contests, which he enjoyed with other frogs, neither he nor any frog he had ever heard of vaulted more than four feet up in the air. He was a little giddy, to say the least – pleased with the view, but quite apprehensive about the sturdiness of this lofty perch. As he began to look from side to side, he noticed that his shoulders seemed much broader than usual, and they seemed much browner than his accustomed green. When he looked down, his mind was frozen for a moment because he could not comprehend what he was seeing: he was either sitting on top of some man's head, or – no … no … he was actually *inside* some man!

His mind was befuddled. He had an attack of vertigo. He was petrified of trying to move. It was easily several minutes before he could even begin to adjust to this metamorphosis. But this was no ordinary frog; indeed, this was no longer a frog at all, but a living, breathing human being with all the experiences and knowledge of a frog, but with the strength, the mobility, the senses, even perhaps the aspirations of a man. One kiss had made this happen. Albeit one kiss from a Princess.

He was very pleasantly surprised at how easily he could move this seemingly "gigantic" frame. He could walk, run, sit, bend, even jump higher than three feet into the air – which was really fun – but a number of problems soon presented themselves. First of all, frogs are not big on clothes, but he knew full well that he could not go walking or jumping around very far without finding something to cover himself. So, he carefully snuck around to the back of the Palace where the trash was collected, and found some passable – if badly mismatched – leggings and a doublet. Secondly, he was exceedingly hungry – and with this new, comparatively short tongue, he quickly gave up on the notion of catching flies in his usual way. Also, the idea of eating the fish that he used to swim with, or any of the animals that he used to talk to, seemed completely abhorrent. He started scouring the forest for fruits and nuts; all new tastes to a frog, and when he found some pears, which immediately became his favorite fruit, he was both delighted and fulfilled.

But there were still more concerns: where would he live now …? and what did a "man" do all day? The pond and the lily pads were certainly not the answer, and even though some of his four-footed friends seemed to recognize him and listen to him when he talked to them, now he had trouble understanding them. He thought he would ease his way up toward the Palace and see if he could learn a bit more about the customs and mores of this new form he now inhabited. On his way, he grabbed a couple of pears and tossed them idly in the air – still marveling at the infinite potential of this human hand he now controlled. As it so often happens, on such seemingly random choices, one's whole life may take on a new direction.

He had gone just beyond the garden gate when a voice cried out to him, "Hey, there, this way, Fool," and a young Guardsman beckoned him to follow. Fred saw no reason for this person to call him a fool, but he was certainly not "fool" enough to argue with a man who had a sword strapped to his belt. So, with more than a little anxiety, he followed him into the Palace and eventually into the Throne Room. He was totally overwhelmed at the size of this room and even more amazed at the extraordinary display of regal garments and jewelry on all the members of the Court. Needless to say, he was struck dumb. But as he was pushed toward the throne and dropped to his knees in a deep bow, his King actually seemed pleased to see him. "Welcome, Fool," the King said, "we have been awaiting your arrival. Pray, entertain us with a quick story," the King continued, "then we will have you shown to your quarters where you can rest from your long journey."

I should explain that the King had been told that a replacement for the Court Jester (who had died of old age last month), would be arriving at the Palace sometime soon: but in fact, none had been found. So, all of the courtiers who had been charged with finding a new jester, were especially happy to see this Fool walk in and, in the days ahead would be more than happy to assist him, how-so-ever they could.

The good news was, that the Fool (for that is what we shall now call him) now had "quarters" to live in and, if he could come up with a quick story, he might have found what he was going to do in this new life. Fortunately, as a frog, he was an excellent listener and quite gregarious, so his memory contained a veritable library of stories told him by various members of the animal kingdom. The one that came first to mind was of a beaver who had great trouble building his dam and a neighboring skunk, whom he greatly disliked, helped him finish it. It's a short story, but the moral is clear: "You never know who might be a friend." The King and all the Court enjoyed the simplicity of the story and the thoughtfulness of its moral.

It came to pass, that the Fool found his home and his vocation because some guardsman thought he could juggle pears. Over the months ahead, he did teach himself to do just that and, with the help of a fox and a monkey, he learned to do a few tricks of legerdemain. As many know, frogs have a very wry sense of humor, so the more sophisticated members of the Court found him greatly amusing. But it was his storytelling that became legendary because he had talked directly with so many animal friends and knew such details as are seldom revealed to any humans. He told "How the Leopard Got His Spots," "How the Alligator Got His Teeth," How the Camel Got His Hump," and literally hundreds more. Many of which have been passed on to other cultures and translated into other languages. The Princess' favorite was "The Princess and The Frog"

Thus, he spent his entire adult life, happy in his work, befriended by almost everyone in Court, and adored by the Princess, whom he never told how instrumental she was in his re-creation. But the story of his origin was told and retold throughout the animal kingdom, so when he would walk through the grounds and neighboring forest, animals of every size and shape would come for the pleasure of being close to him. Cats – not so much.

Years later, when the King became ill, he called the aging Fool to him, presented him with a bag of gold coins, and told him the time had come for him to retire and pursue whatever path he would. So, the Fool bid the Princess LeeAnne and all the Court a humble farewell and set off over the mountains to see what might lie in the next valley. There he settled into a comfortable clearing that contained a pond not too dissimilar from the one he knew so well, and was soon caring for any animals that brought him their complaints – and he was very content.

As fate would have it, a young Princess named Miriam walked into his glen one day. They ate his simple fare together; they came to know each other in a very special way and eventually became more than just friends. It came to pass, that in a spirit of pure love, the Princess kissed him ... and he turned back into a frog.

He sits, even now, on the loveliest of lily pads in this loveliest of ponds in this loveliest of glens and contemplates, with both amazement and amusement – the mysterious circle of life ... and the power of a single kiss.

THE END

Addenda

The Best Beast

On the shore of lake Mogambo,

In the hills of Ungeroo,

Lived the dreaded beast Throngolum

Who could bite a man in two.

Though seldom seen in daylight,

One who did was heard to swear:

"Twice as tall as a Jugalon

And hairier than a bear."

His teeth were gnarled and greenish-brown,

His feet like stumps of trees,

His arms as firm as castle walls,

His hands hung to his knees.

The sounds he made were wild and fierce

And echoed like a drum.

Though some decried it held more pain,

"Like he bit off your thumb."

He was not as swift as the Scattercat

Nor tall as a banyan tree,

But fast enough to catch a horse,

Which he ate by two's and threes.

———

Two valleys away in a verdant glen

Lived a kindly Bugalabet.

She was tiny and neat and so very sweet

And friends with whomever she met.

When first she heard of the Throngolum

She was nearly brought to tears,

For she knew in her heart that not anyone

Was as bad as what reached her ears.

So she wrote him a note, with a daisy inside,

And sent it off by a dove.

Her message came to the Throngolum

As if from heaven above.

She praised his strength and honesty,

And marveled at his size.

Often she heard that he was so brave

And had the kindest eyes.

She knew in her heart, he was misunderstood

And was kindly and smart and true blue.

She honestly thought all bad reports

Were sure to be untrue.

She hoped he took good care of himself

And brushed his teeth each day.

She warned him also to stay out of drafts,

And keep the flies away.

———

The Throngolum was so amazed
That anyone could care,
That he brushed his teeth and cut his nails,
And combed his mangy hair.
He vowed to change his ways that day,
And not eat another man.
He learned to write to the Bugalabet
And told her of his plan.
He would try to be kind to all he met
Whether they large or small,
He would keep his cave neat, not overeat,
And bathe in the Spring and the Fall.
He would try not to do what she said not to do,
And care for her all of his life;
He'd even stop eating the horses he loved,
If she would just come be his wife.

Who knew that a single letter could bring
This tale to a happy end?
To change the mighty Throngolum
From a fiend into a friend.

THE END